Thomas Woolner

Pygmalion

Thomas Woolner

Pygmalion

ISBN/EAN: 9783337405670

Printed in Europe, USA, Canada, Australia, Japan

Cover: Foto ©Andreas Hilbeck / pixelio.de

More available books at **www.hansebooks.com**

PYGMALION

BY

THOMAS WOOLNER

London
MACMILLAN AND CO.
1881

TO MY WIFE

Alice Gertrude

I OFFER THIS VISION OF THE PAST

CONTENTS.

PRELUDE.

WHO can extract its secret from the rose,
    Or tell us why the violet glows ;
Or tulips, why in mystic stripes they flame,
    Why crimson poppies burn in shame ?

Who shall expound why man with open fate
    Chooses for partner ash-faced Hate ;
When shy, soft, willing Love, deliciously,
    In warmth and smiles stands blushing by?

Who can say why bold rulers love to lie,
    And mean ones love to mystify ?
By what perversity of logic led,
    When truth would stand in better stead !

B

)

That Love should turn from Love and paradise
    To riches, vanity, or vice;
Barter the glory of a life's content,
    Is marvel and bewilderment!

But I will leave to moralists the Why
    Things unseen are not seen, and try
Wing'd venture into days remote and old,
    Till I the mystery unfold

How passion deep, and Aphrodite's aid,
    Resolved to life that wondrous Maid,
Pygmalion wrought in marble, by the stress
    Of worship, to pure loveliness.

BOOK I.

PYGMALION ardent-eyed, of eager speech
Which even closest friends misunderstood,
Was sorely troubled with a passionate hope
To bring the Gods' own language, sculpture,
        down
For mortal exaltation.
                        Thus mused he :

Men made in marble look but men, no more ;
But Gods in sculpture are immortal powers
To whom we kneel helplessly lost in awe.
Man wrought the men and also wrought the Gods.
In making Gods doth Pallas give device,
And Hermes put strange cunning in the hand,
And Hyperion fill the eyes with light,
Such greatness shows when mortals work for
        Gods ?

Thus wandered he in mazes : when perchance
He caught a seeming clue and onward strove,
Sudden a blank impossibility
Closed his advance and drove him wide again;
Till effort breeding failure sickened him,
Who, like a squirrel in a turning cage,
Found himself where he was for all his pains.

By watchful constancy of tenderness,
By the melodious pathos of his voice,
And his refulgent presence day by day,
Pygmalion charmed his mateless mother's home.
Nor could her love have spared him, save for
    high
And godlike quest, or service to the state.
Mindful, in woman's fondness, of the tall
Lithe form, smooth sinewy arms, those eyes so
    full
Of gracious light and sweet attent, came back
The days agone ; when, with her lord alone,
Safe in the strength of his nerved arms' defence,

Along the shore they saw sun-smitten waves,
Casting back light from their long shoulder lines,
Plunge shattering the beach ; a whispered hiss
Following the roar in thralled monotony.
And when on shady forest bank he lay
Tranced at her feet ; a plectrum in his hand,
By tuneful touch urging the song he sang
To her as fairest of all womanhood.
Or, when their city thronged the chariot race,
A meteor he flashed by, his eyes alight,
His horses' eyes alight, to victory:
When all the matrons, all the maidens turned
Straightway on her to gaze !

                Thus with the past
The blessed present blent, till life became
One rounded thankfulness and prayer the Gods
Would hold it whole and scathless to the end.

   Beside her household slaves, and those who
     won
Their freedom by their worth, twelve noble maids

Did suit and service to uphold her state
And learn from her the management of home.
All fit observances of time and place ;
All secrets of the loom ; skill in the use
Of warp and weft ; their textures various ;
Colours unchangeable, to each one fit.
Of herbs : knowledge of food and cordial drinks :
Pastimes, and exercises : when was best
To lave their lovely bodies in the sea,
And race, with garments looped, across the lawn.
Whatever made them prudent, strong, and fair,
Worthy to wed with heroes and to rear
A race of children bold and beautiful.

No greatest painter by the Gods beloved,
Painting their deeds on their own Temple walls
Gave more devotion to the forms that grew
Day after day beneath his subtle hand,
Than she in fashioning her maidens' lives
Unto their fullest nature : each one's gifts
Brightening with use, expanding in the press

Of loving rivalry and sympathy,
Working together under wise control.

No daughters could love more, or be more
    loved.
Unlike, but all as one when bending low
They gave to her the simultaneous " Hail"
Of morning salutation.

                        Phœbe, dark,
High-born and of most lofty vein, disdained
Belief in meanness, save as some defect
Strange and unblamable, like stench of fox.
Calliope her sworn friend next, who might
Be sister, so alike in voice and ways.
Eos the tender : great blue timid eyes,
Fleetest of foot ; of such an easy pace
When at her utmost speed and seen afar
She looked a drifting cloud.   Then Myrrha who
Would play and sing of dragons, demigods,
And fields of blood : which, calm Ianthe
    thought,

Might well be changed for men and pastorals,
Corn-laughing harvests, flocks, and dulcet grapes.
But gay Metharme doubted ; vowed that blood
Was manly ; that foul dragon's blood enriched
The soil and brought forth heavier crops ; that
     men
Were born to slay and dragons to be slain.
Euphrosyne would rather sing of light,
How the God made our world afresh each morn
With new-born flowers, new strength to man
     and beast,
Then smiled in dazzling splendours his farewell.
But Thisbe, olive-hued, whose Sire had come
From far-off sunny lands, wondered what dark
Drear fate was on the God he dwelt each night
With darkness and with Death !   Or can it be
He goes to lands unknown and shines on men
And other maidens at their tasks as here ?
A wealth of sumptuous grace was Smyrna,
     who
Murmured to stately Clytie " Dreams again :

Our Thisbe's Eastern dreams!"   "Nay, Western
    say,"
Cried sprightly Neis, " for thence the God
    departs !"
Aglaia meek, gentle in all her ways,
Took truest note of every duty charged
And kindly aiding was beloved of all.

Each maiden had her well-appointed work,
Either to weave; to measure seeds, or oil;
Direct the corn-grinding ; stow safe the fruits
Sun-dried erewhile, or in wild honey kept.
Some cleared the garment-presses to espy
Amid care-woven wool, linen, or silks
If moth made havoc.   Numbers variable
Of slaves, or women freed, suited to needs,
Obeyed each maid's command ; doing all rough
And lower labour : but the sacred Gods
No slave on pain of high displeasure dares
Finger : Aglaia, she whose white hands fell
Softly as snowflakes on a windless day,

Reverently, with lightest zephyr touch
Of swandown plume, beats off the summer dust.

A ruler born ; tho' mistress of each art,
Wisely the matron at no labour toiled,
But held a watchful eye on every maid,
With guidance here and gentle pressure there,
By hint or look, by tone, and words of cheer
Kept the mixed household one harmonious
    whole.

BOOK II.

BEYOND a cloud of pines the chambers stood
Where toiled Pygmalion.   Loftily they rose
And widely stretched ; by the curved pathway
    grew
Laurel alternately with honoured bay
On either side in pairs : between each pair
An oleander gorgeous in the bloom
Of rosy light gladdened the massive green :
While flanking all gigantic cypresses
And olives huge in gnarled antiquity
Made an elysium for the birds of heaven.

It was Pygmalion's wont to rise at dawn,
Reach the lone shore and plunge into the sea ;
And after joyful buffet with the waves
Begin his labours with the singing day.

At times he wandered far along the sands
And drank the radiant beams as from the
      waves
They flashed in light and laughter to his feet ;
Wondering how man with such a heritage
In splendours manifold, his own each day
For ever, passed that span 'twixt birth and
      death
In hate, and wild beast clutchings after gain
Through wild beast slaughters ; giving scantily
To love, and loveliness, and kindly acts !

Or he would range the forest solitudes
To meditate by what new feats of art
That ever-present beauty haunting him
Could be in substance bound and manifest ;
And how the life that beamed in all he saw
Could be made beam to others as to him.

These lapses from close labour nerved his
      will,

Which, quickening half-born dreams and
    thoughts obscure
To living truths, gave him the strength he
    craved
Whereby to animate the forms he wrought
With nature's varied movement; pause and
    play
Of impulse: complex outwardly in strain
And laxity alert.   Armed with this power
The damp impressible clay glanced into light
Along the tendons' length; hardened to bone;
And tightened straightway into comely shape
Beneath his certain touch.   Hard marble
    changed,
In softened shadows rounding tenderly
To firm elastic life : and what anon
Was but as chaos beamed a new delight
More lasting than all beauty born of man.

    Pygmalion now was working to reveal
The wonder of great Aphrodite's birth.

How raged Lycurgus at the proffered gift
Of Dionysus.   How Prometheus bound
Was spared the vulture's beak by Heracles.
And how rebellious Titans overthrown
Writhed shattered under Zeus omnipotent.
These were the deeds he conned, and strove to
      show
On four great walls of marble pure and white.

CYTHEREA.

Uprisen from the sea when Cytherea,
Shining in primal beauty, paled the day,
The wondering waters hushed.   They yearned
      in sighs
That shook the world : tumultuously heaved
To a great throne of azure laced with light
And canopied in foam to grace their Queen.
Shrieking for joy came Oceanides,
And swift Nereides rushed from afar
Or clove the waters by.   Came eager-eyed
Even shy Naiades from inland streams,

With wild cries headlong darting thro' the
    waves ;

And Dryads from the shore stretched their lorn
    arms.

While hoarsely sounding heard was Triton's
    shell ;

Shoutings uncouth; sudden, bewildered sounds;

And the innumerable splashing feet

Of monsters gambolling around their God,

Forth shining on a seahorse, fierce, and finned.

Some bestrode fishes glinting dusky gold,

Or angry crimson, or chill silver bright ;

Others jerked fast on their own scaly tails ;

And seabirds, screaming upwards either side,

Wove a vast arch above the Queen of Love,

Who, gazing on this multitudinous

Homaging to her beauty, laughed :

                    She laughed

The soft delicious laughter that makes mad ;

Low warblings in the throat that clench man's
    life

Tighter than prison bars.

                Then swayed a breath
Of odorous rose and scented myrtle mixed,
That toyed the golden radiance round her brows
To wavy flames.   When lo ! sweet murmurings
Spread sudden silence on that gathered host !
And, as sped arrows to their mark ; as bees
Drop promptly on the honey'd flower, as one
Shone the three daughters of Eurynome,
Aglaia, and Thalia ; each an arm
In reverence taking fondled tenderly ;
Then pressed their blushing cheeks against her
      breasts :
And loved Euphrosyne, scarcely less fair
Than Cytherea's self, lay her white length
Kissing the sacred feet.

                Such honour paid
The powers of nature to the power of Love,
Creation's longed-for Wonder sprung to life !

Now, as a man lifts up a little child,

Placing it down where he would have it walk,

The wave of mighty azure forward driven

By magic impulse sheer in downward slope

Fell, then drawn backward sank, and was no
     more ;

Leaving the Goddess on her Cyprian coast.

And when her feet first touched the trembling
     sand,

She fired awakened Earth's remotest veins

To strange ethereal ecstasies ; as birds

Brighten to clamour by the fires of morn.

   Thus to Pygmalion beamed the wondrous
     Birth ;

And this in pure immortal marble he

Laboured to show ; bound by those rules of
     Art

The Wise had found inexorably fixed.

DIONYSUS.

When Dionysus, flushed triumphantly

C

From Indian deeds, rich-bronzed by Indian
    suns,
And riotous in delightful lustihood,
First touched the shore of Thrace ; around him
    thronged
His large-limbed, cymbal-clashing nymphs ;
    rough fauns
Braying horn trumpets ; ruddy satyrs danced,
Clicking their hard hoofs on the harder rocks :
Weak-kneed Silenus, puffing, on both sides
Upheld by grinning slaves, who plied the cup,
Wherein two nymphs squeezed juice of dusky
    grapes.
Bright girls and agile youths curvetting wild
On leopards, bitted, straining gilded reins,
Nigh touched the God, lolling on tiger huge,
Silent of footfall, tawny flamed and striped ;
He with his ivied spear pointing the way.
Stout baby boys, bestriding frisky goats,
Clutched fast their horns when arching up to
    butt ;

Rolling each other under perilous paws.

Behind walked modest maids and men sedate

Whose charge it was to bear the nurseling
    vines.

. In logbuilt palace grim Lycurgus, King,

Scornful of corn and oil and every fruit,

Ate flesh himself had slain.   He hunted sure,

Tracking his prey by signs to certain fate.

Came unto him the din : first faintly heard ;

Soon swelling into loud uproar that burned

The blood within him to a warlike rage ;

When, seizing nearest weapons, head unhelmed,

Clattering spear on shield, he rushed without

And to his people shouted vehemently.

Hastily arming, wondering, on they came,

Obedient to the call ; fast they formed rank ;

Led by their King fast strode to meet the
    God.

When Dionysus saw this threatening front

Advance and pause, the King's eyes darting
    fires
Of anger under knitted brows, before
He put his helmet on and fastened it ;
Lightly he left the tiger's back, to meet
And offer make the King, in accents soft
Of nurseling plants that seasonably would grow
Abundant grapes and load his land with wealth,
Thro' which his people might by interchange
Take toll of others' best ; and thus increase
Their gladness : so, by multiplying needs
Quicken their energies to wider range
Of action ; growing greater with the march
Of timely circumstance, that ever aids
All willing workers towards some statelier end.
    Whereat Lycurgus smiling ghastliwise :
This then your plea for bursting on my lands
Without leave asked ! To give my men a boon
Which swells them in their own esteem to Gods,
But leaves them beasts, without clear-sighted-
    ness

Of beasts.   We are content to feed on flesh
Provided by the Gods : but not content
To scrape, and scratch, and dig the earth for
    food,
Like slave that knoweth not the use of arms.
Fruit is for babes ; flesh for the teeth of man.
Behold your bloat Silenus !   What unstrung
The sinews of his knees, that scarcely bear
The over-burdened weight above ?   To steal
Man's strength, and give instead unwieldy size :
Is this your boon !

                  With other states we will
Not deal save with our swords and spears.
    And last,
As touching this exalted life you vaunt,
How fared it with Damascus, good old King ?
Who would have saved his people from this
    taint
That fouls the blood to weakness, sickness,
    death ;
But you corrupted them ; and him you slew !

How of his skin ?   Was it to leather tanned
To hold your grape juice stored ! Owls ! Owls !
    I say,
Owls !   And down spears !
            Then, as a sudden gust
On corn, hurtling fell down the spears as one
To deadly point of menace.
            Shifting round
His wolfskin ; right arm free forth leaped the
    King
And cried the charge.
            Stepping some paces back,
Nearly as Powers who know the future can
Be struck amazed at acts of mortal man
An instant in immortal sorrow gazed
The God surprised.   Then from his features
    flashed
A lurid lightning glare portending doom.
Lowering his lance whilom at shivering poise
He moved stern-visaged towards the ocean
    cliffs.

Now whistling shrill, winged death in volleys
    flew ;
Now charged the press of spears in level line ;
Now crashed the storm in shouts and shrieks
    and cries ;
Huddling confused they clambered interlocked
Hindering escape.   Quick-eyed Lycurgus sent
Swift-footed bowmen to outrun and head
Inland the rout before they made the sea.
    When Dionysus saw Necessity,
Before whose presence Zeus himself must bow,
Oppose his cherished plan, and Hope saw not,
Scaling an ocean crag he cried aloud

Woe to the mortal who assaults a God !
Fear; palsied madness; some outrageous death !
Come the Erinyes soon : I hear their wings !

Then at Lycurgus hurling his green spear
Thro' metal shield and right uplifted arm ;
He plunged down headlong in the plunging
    waves,

Where Thetis, by the mightiest Gods beloved,
Calming the waters saved the God from hurt.

Thus saw Pygmalion Dionysus' gift
Roughly rejected by Lycurgus, King.
And this in pure immortal marble he
Laboured to show; bound by those rules of Art
The Wise had found inexorably fixed.

PROMETHEUS.

Prometheus lived not wholly God nor man,
But nobler far than all the Gods of heaven,
Save one, Pallas Athena, whom he loved ;
And she, The Wise One, loved Prometheus.   But
Not as the love of mortals was her love,
Nor loves of other Gods.

                  He, Titan, dared
Encourage man against the harsh decrees
Of Zeus, who minded they should cease to live,
Being base, and restless, asking, helpless things.
As one decrees whose tillage has been cropped
With seeds and roots unsuited to the soil.

But brooding pity great Prometheus moved
At men's poor efforts to endure a war
Opposing adverse fate.   He saw their lands
Smiling in ripening corn and tended fruits
Ravaged by one great storm to uselessness :
And when the suppliants prayed almighty Zeus
For help, no answer came but blank despair.
Saw swarming hosts, lacking one ray to light
Their blindness, close in deadly strife, till soaked
In blood, and thinned by loss, their argument
Is solved in desolation.   Famines saw
Conjunct with foulness breeding pestilence ;
Floods overspreading uncontrollable,
Sweep them to sudden and resistless ruin.

He saw their anguish. As they had no choice
In their own birth, they were perforce released
Of shend or blame in their wild ways forlorn :
Where ignorance paced by them step for step,
With chance and danger dogging at their heels.

Prometheus, he of all the Heavenly-born,

Alone felt sympathy for wretched man.
By grief emboldened he Athena sought
And kneeling to her Presence made his boon :

One ray to guide these gadding wanderers ;
One spark of fire divine that they may melt
Their metals, bake their corn, and roast their flesh ;
For you best know, O Goddess, your clear word
Brings scattered many into strength compact,
And turns the front of blind antagonism.
    Grant you the fire and I myself will show
How metal red shall run like melted wax
And harden into spears.   Hard must it be
For pigmies with their clubs, and flint-made
        blades
Fighting with lions, boars, and savage bulls ;
And hard to eat their flesh, like lions, raw ;
Their tasteless, unbaked corn.
                    The Titan's zeal
Made great Athena smile : amused, she asked
If next his prayer importune would for bees,

Which store their food and also eat it raw :
Or if for goats, to arm their horns and feet
That they may war with lions.

　　　　　　　　　Bending low,
He looked so meek and sad : he could not
　　smile ;
He spoke not ; eyes alone making appeal
Once more.

　　　　　　Not love of man, but from deep love
Of him Prometheus she her promise gave
Of counsel : promised he should snatch the fire
From torch of Eros, thunderbolt of Zeus,
Or from the car of Helios seize a spark.

　　And when at length thro' fears unspeakable,
Tho' shadowed by Athena's dreadful shield,
He snatched the fire and brought it down to
　　man,
The wrath of Zeus was thundered thro' the hills,
And shook the base of heaven.　So fiercely
　　flew
The fire throughout mankind, he saw no less

Than deluge overwhelming the whole world
Could quench it now.   And as relentless Fate
Decreed this could not be, his rage he turned
Against the godlike Thief, and punished him
With pain more dire and unendurable
Than e'er was known either by God or man.

　　After Prometheus had for ages borne
The tearing of the demon's eagle beak:
Whether remembrance of high service done
When the leagued Giants made their huge
　　　　assault ;
Or tired to hear his yells of agony ;
Or that he from the Titan's lips had learned
To dread the offspring of his Thetis loved ;
Great Zeus at length relenting sent his Son,
Strong Heracles, to slay the fiend, and set
Prometheus bold, the mighty Titan, free.

　　The feathered demon flapping in the dust,
The Sufferer delivered.   The wild joy

That Naiades brought down from mountain
    streams :
Dryads and Nymphs with long uplifted arms
Shouting their exultation he was free !
This was a scene that charged Pygmalion's soul :
And this in pure immortal marble he
Laboured to show ; bound by those rules of Art
The Wise had found inexorably fixed.

ZEUS.

   Ere the omnipotence of Zeus was known
By every Power of Earth, and Sea, and Air ;
The Titans, who had sometime been a law
Each to himself, bore the outrageous load,
Enforced authority !   Their ancient joy
Was gone ; their old prerogative to lounge
Through the long sunshine ; or to work at will.
The galling need to worship what they loathed;
Or seem to worship, which they loathed yet
    more ;
Made brooding hate grow deadlier day by day,

And deepen in the dreamings of the night,
When the mysterious fires of darkness burned
Watching the fates of Titans and of Gods ;
Till anger burst in flame ; and all as one
Were bent on war to battle for their own.

   Great Zeus beholding vapour rise to cloud
And thicken dark to threatening storm among
The furious Titans, to Athena spoke
Asking her aid and counsel in the strife
Impending.   If on Mount Olympus they
Should wait assault ; or to the plain descend
And crush the Giants there.

                      Athena thought
It best the Titans came to waste their strength
Climbing the steep and overhanging crags ;
For even Titans scale not heights as these
Without fatigue ; and when fatigued more light
The work to slay them.   Help she would
     demand
Of skilled Prometheus, so that he may smooth

Our heights more inaccessible to grip
Of feet and clasp of hands : and, Titan born,
He knows their fighting ways.
                              The Thunderer smiled
Benignly that his might redoubled through
His Daughter, Wise, and bowed his head
    divine.

    The secret purpose glowing in his soul,
Unwearied, wrought Prometheus.   For he had
With sure fore-knowledge seen the Giants'
    doom,
And hoped by serving the Olympian Gods
To claim for wage a spark of Heaven's fire.
Without this hope, even his love for Her,
Pallas Athena, scarce could make him front
In death-determined contest his own kin,
Playmates of yore, rough, and untamable.
But for his pigmies, who fast multiplied,
And waxed in force with every watched-for
    chance ;

He was invincibly resolved to win
The vital spark by which alone they might
Be lifted from the brutes.

                  Therefore toiled he
Incessantly ; shaping huge blocks to fit
One on the other close, and side by side.
Not straight, as falls a stone, was built the
     wall,
But sloping, as a spear that stands at rest ;
The outward face against the danger smooth
By chiselling square and true.   When piled a
     height
He knew inviolable, Prometheus, now
Served by the Cyclops three, in caldrons vast,
With fires of roaring forest trees, that breathed
A thousand years of sun, hewn short to logs,
Rough metals melted, white, and red, and gold,
And poured the burning splendour from above,
Filling up every joint and crevice down
To the foundations on the living rock
In solid mass compact ; which stretched across

From mountain wall to wall.   While sheer
    behind
Hung cliffs, accessible alone to flight
Of eagles, or the wings of drifting storm,
Leaving but one way for the huge assault.

   Since the great Earth from Chaos first was
    hatched,
And fledged herself in wonders sun by sun,
And moon by moon, no wonder held the light,
Filling the day with such resplendent awe,
As when the Titans armed with oaks, up-
    wrenched,
And lumps of rock, enormous, forward moved
In even paces towards the huge assault :
And the Olympian Gods awaiting them
In range for action !
                 Brighter than clear noon
Shone Zeus ; within whose hands quivered the
    bolts
Of thunder-fire flashing impatiently.

                       D

While on his right Pallas Athena stood

Well nigh as tall : her dreadful shield be-
    hind

Her thrown, its horror toward the cliffs : Her
    spear

Looked a fixed star emitting baleful light.

He who made Ocean tame, Poseidon, great

Earth-shaker, by his Brother's side, aloft

His ocean sceptre held as he would crash

The rock-bound world.   Ares his whole length
    lay

Watching the Titans' march.   And hovering
    round

The bird of Zeus hung darkly over all.

   Their shouts uniting made a howl that
    mocked

Olympian thunders, or deep ocean's rage

At utmost press of storm ; the Giants' rush

Began in breathless climb, in desperate
    leap ;

Their monstrous sizes looming on the heights
Like moving worlds.   Some stooping tried to
    reach
Help to their brothers.   Hindering fragments
    some
Tore off to fill and bridge a rift profound :
Vainly all shoulders join to heave aside
A mountain mass.
                Severely smiled the Gods
At useless efforts, seeing them descend
Adventuring afresh.
                Then Pallas, winged,
Half fiend, uprose scanning around, and saw
A path whereby the plain at length was free
Reaching unbroken the Olympian wall.
    Awhile the Titans panted ; their tried hearts
In throbs of muffled thunder beating doom.
Vast crags upheaving, brandishing whole oaks,
With every root upwrenched ; they with a roar
Like earthquake, in stupendous bounds, their
    weight

Shaking the earth that seemed with them to
    move,
Rushed on their fate making the huge assault.

  At this uproar serenely gazed the Gods
Expectant.   Striding forth, Enceladus
Hurled a great rock aimed at the brows of
    Zeus,
Whose bolt in mid air shivered it to dust,
Dashing its fragments in the Giants' sight;
Their rocky masses, now thrown wide and wild,
Fell harmless.
          Then by Styx, the Thunderer swore,
This soon should end, and let his lightnings
    play.
His bolts scored ghastly chasms through their
    flesh;
And death flew in the shafts of Heracles;
While Ares stamped his foot and shook his
    shield,
And thro' the nearest sent his joyful lance.

Pallas, the Giant-fiend, seizing a rock,
Winged his way upward with the fell intent
To crush the brain of Zeus, whose eagle saw,
And, darting high, swooped on the Giant's nape,
Tearing his head.

             To free himself the fiend
Let fall the stone, which struck a Titan dead,
And, mad for pain, alighted on the space
Held by the Gods : where, neither pain nor hate
Glared through his eyes when on Athena fixed
He at her garment clutched with vulture claws;
She, drawing back a pace, regarded him.
She did not face him with her Gorgon shield.
She did not frown. · Her look was worse than
    death,
When, poising spear, the irresistible,
She crashed him through the brain.

                With sudden strength,
Almost of Heracles, Silenus dragged
The carcass to the wall and rolled it down.

    Sprang the lost Giants on the lifeless bulk ;

Some kneeling down for others to mount higher,

Hoping their wrath might scale the hopeless
wall.

And lo !   By frantic bounds, two hard-strained
hands

The wall grasped tight !   Swifter than falcon's
speed

The blade of Ares clove the knotted wrists ;

And dropped the vast bulk down the heaven-
built wall.

   The ruined Titan falling, with him bore

His clambering brethren in a tangled mass

That burst the earth up like a splash of
waves

With thund'rous sound, and momentary night

Of dust.   In heaps uncouth the Giants lay

Slaughtered, or writhing from the huge assault.

   Thus saw Pygmalion Titans overthrown ;

Some writhing yet among the huddled dead :

While Zeus above, His Powers on either side,

Stood with His ready bolts omnipotent.

And this in pure immortal marble he

Laboured to show ; bound by those rules of
    Art

The Wise had found inexorably fixed.

BOOK III.

IT was Ianthe's duty every noon
To bring Pygmalion bread, and fruit, and wine,
And place them in the chamber where he
    wrought.
At times she saw he heeded not ; so bound
Unto the dimly formed uncertain things
His active chisel laboured to release
From their confinement in the marble world.
She dared not break the spell : and quietly
Returned unnoticed. But more often he
Graciously owned the care and gentleness
She day by day bestowed. Then would she
    pour
For him the wine : offer the bread and fruit :
And maybe tarry to behold his skill
Translating into substance visible

Love's tenderness, or passion's smouldering
    depths.
How shaped Aglaia's cheek against the charm
Of Aphrodite's breast. How the sharp lines
Of agony Prometheus must endure,
Tortured less cruelly his spacious brow :
Or gloomed the shades of power more deeply
    calm
And terrible within the eyes of Zeus.
Well pleased to watch from time to time the Gods,
And others, cleared of their embarrassment.

    His Mother with Ianthe came one day
In azure June to watch her son at work ;
For she had fears unceasing toil might fret,
If left unminded, her Pygmalion's strength.
She would press on him nourishment, and plead
He took more rest and sportful exercise.

    They found him mounted higher than the
    ground

Working at Cytherea's smile.   His floor
Was overspread with mat, the Matron's slaves
Wove of green rushes, soft of pith, that he
Be spared unnecessary noise, even noise
Of his own footsteps, in those rarer moods
When thought is striving to complete itself.

Pausing, the Matron and Ianthe watched
Admiringly, the chisel's dainty play
Soften the valley 'twixt the cheek and mouth,
Sweeten the laughter rippling thro' the lips,
And fine the chin to rarer witchery.

They might have waited long, for he was
      lost
In Aphrodite's laugh and loveliness,
As they were well-nigh lost regarding him.
But prudently the Mother curbed her joy
At her son's handcraft ; and solicitous
That her main errand proved not profitless,
Signed to Ianthe, who poured out the wine,

And asked,

       Will you drink wine, my Lord ?

He turned,
Gazing as one awakened from a dream,
Eyes on the maiden fixed.   Descending, then
He to his Mother bending reverently,
Kissed her loved hands.

       Ianthe, drink will I !
Without libation would I drain a cup
That should Silenus shame commanded by
One so imperiously meek !   But now
You looked as a great Hebe meet to fill
His goblet for high Zeus sitting enthroned !

Moved in the pure white blossom of her cheeks
A tinge of rose : taking the cup she placed
It down ; then brought him bread and fruit.

       He cried,

O mother, give me your assent and I
Will carve Ianthe as she stood erewhile
Pouring the wine, a Hebe, child of Zeus
And Hera, pouring nectar for the God!
In her deep eyes there shone an upward awe
As though she gazed at Zeus gazing at her.

  The matron smiled, and said, if Hebe he
Must carve, Eos the tender was most fit;
Being of lighter form, and what would seem
To men the figure of immortal youth.

  Eos were well, my Mother, were I bound
To make her fill the cup for Heracles,
Or her own brother Ares.   But I mean
To make her serving Zeus her Father, who,
Throwing his thunders makes Olympus shake;
Ianthe's gaze alone for him is fit.

    Your work is hard, my Son; your health
        will fail
If worked to overstrain.

Fear not for me

O Mother!   Labour in its fullest force

Heightens the blood ; gives to the limbs their
strength,

And scales by storm the noblest heights of
thought.

It is the daily cark and constant dread

That fret the body down to wretchedness.

But feel this arm, and judge if that be weak !

She laid her hand upon his lissom arm,

Fine on its surface as the myrtle flower,

Hard as the shoulder of the proudest horse,

First in a chariot race.   Though thus assured,

The Mother felt his shot beyond her range.

Now daily came Ianthe to repeat

The posture for Pygmalion which he chose

For youthful Hebe when she filled the cup

Of Zeus.   Hard was the Maiden's task, for she

Flinched not at tingling nerves and throbbing
pulse ;

Tho' dizzy oft from the continual strain
Of keeping motionless.   He, all absorbed,
Regarded her but as a beauteous shape
Aiding him in the Godlike counterfeit,
Unconscious what she felt.   Amazed each day
By fresh perfections dawning, he, each day,
More resolutely toil'd.   The gracefulness
And pride of her long rounded throat, his hands
Changed into awkwardness by mimicry.
The arches of her shoulders !   Could he touch
On curves so exquisitely drooped, their sheen
Of movement tremulous !   In despair he sighed,
Avowing it impossible for hand
To trace the lines in full variety
Throughout the space of that majestic breast;
Of dignity so peerless that if clad
In the great Virgin's golden armour scales
They would but seem a suitable defence.

Ianthe, calmly perfect, stood complete
In youthful strength, whose easy negligence

Of varying grace baffled the captive sight
To trace her beauties thro' the play and flush
Of bounding health exulting in its home!

Though uncomplainingly she bore the strain
Pleased was Ianthe when a slanting ray
Brightening Prometheus as he lay enchained
Proclaimed the noon.
                            One day on going back
Caught was she half-way in the curving path,
By gust so boisterous she needs must stop,
And battling with her fluttering folds, was blown
Half round, and chancing saw Pygmalion stand
Within the doorway shade regarding her.
    Delightfulness ran trembling through her
        limbs.
An unfamiliar music beat her heart!
 She moved without her feet.
                            Metharme cried

Cheeks apple-blossoms; and how rough your hair,

Ianthe !

     Yes, the wind against me beat
So forcibly I scarce could make my way.

  We saw the struggling. Well knew Boreas
The sweetness of a wrestle with the charms
Of one so well endowed. Your garments he
Plucked at so wildly I began to dread
We might become like old Tiresias
When great Athena bathed !

         Metharme, hush :
Pray hush ! The Matron urged ; seeing how
  prompt
Her Maidens' titter at the quaint conceit,
Ianthe robbed and vanquished to her own
White beauty bare, in native comeliness.
  Ianthe spoke not but the blush remained.

  Doves softly cooing murmurs musical
Gladdened unseen the darksome cloud of pines :
Below bright-hued innumerable wings

Carried love messages from flower to flower.

For Spring's outstretching fingers nearly
    touched

The Summer's welcoming hands. Pygmalion's
    work

On Hebe's statue now was nearly done ;

Tho' yet her features lacked that splendid gaze

Of worship which Pygmalion saw, or thought

He once saw in Ianthe's face, and fired

The passionate belief he could present

Immortal Hebe pouring for the God.

   While looking on Ianthe's comely sway

Of body, and her shapely limbs, ofttimes

His spirit sickened hopelessly.

                         The way

Her large and dainty fingers held the cup

Would make the taste of nectar more divine.

The arched perfection of her supple feet

Might stay the flight of Hermes to be kissed !

These seemed to him as unattainable

E

As flight of lark singing in deepest blue
To creeping unwinged things.   But now, alas !
He could not through her features penetrate
And find the glory which he knew must dwell
In Hebe's brow.
                         Perfect was her face.
From dark gray eyes of dawn the gazer's sight
Would tenderly on her pure forehead rest.
Her nostrils breathed a purer air than Earth's;
And the clear curves that marked her drooping
        mouth
Would seem of discontent, save for the two
Full roses midway kissing.   Half distraught,
Remembering how, as from a mystic dream,
He woke and saw Ianthe, as she stood
Holding the wine, believed the splendid gaze
He saw, a remnant of his dream, and not
Ianthe's own, as he thought heretofore.

   Awhile at this perplexed, a tremor crept
Upon him, for he feared that never more
That gaze, as at a God, should he behold ;

And mayhap, the bright touch of life divine
Be wanting to his Hebe.

Therefore he,
Having the Maiden's features fashioned true,
Used them no more: but down the inmost
　　depths
His memory could sound sought the lost light
To quicken Hebe's eyes, as though she gazed
At Zeus upon his throne gazing on her.

　Now that Ianthe was no longer there
A part of daily labour, sometimes came
The sense of want, or loss, as if the day
Were chill with clouds. The habit had so
　　grown
Of looking to her form for guidance sure,
Often he found himself at gaze upon
The empty platform where she sometime stood
Earnestly bent on giving him all aid.
And when at noon Ianthe came, the clouds
Vanished to nothing in the golden prime.

BOOK IV.

LONGED not Prometheus for the fire of heaven
Wherewith to solace miserable man,
More vehemently than sought Pygmalion
The spark to flash his Hebe into life.
His utmost stopped at failure ; spent, he felt
Powerless, helpless, if unaided now
By gracious favour of immortal Love.

   The sunshine in his soul ; his tranquil home ;
His work, making the high Olympian Gods
Known to his fellows by their mighty deeds,
Left not Pygmalion hapless ; though his wish
Strove ever onwards, urged unceasingly
By hope and growing powers.
                    Willing to know
How others would respect his Hebe's form,

He asked his Mother to bring all her Maids
To pass their judgment.
                    In their stateliness
Processional, the Maidens came in threes,
And pairs ; some cast long loving arms around
Each other's waists and shoulders.   Hand in
      hand
Walked some ; and some half loitering plucked
      at sprigs
Or flowers, or listened tranced the nightingale
Warbling pathetic secrets all may hear
And few may understand.   The Matron last
With calm Ianthe came.
                    Advanced, her son
Had come to meet them in the curving path.
He hailed them gaily; vowed the blooming Hours,
Or the tall Graces with the Muses nine,
Marching together had not looked more fair !

Entering, the Matron and her Maidens ranged
Themselves at fitting distance ; mute awhile

Ere the twelve-voiced home oracle pronounced.
Some on the mat, rushwoven, sat them down ;
While others lounged on seats : some leaned
    against
The farthest wall, holding their heads aslant
And hands in movement, conned the work by
    parts.

    Phoebe spoke first, and thought the statue
    good :
True to Ianthe's stately grace. A new
And splendid Temple were a fitting home.
    Like our Ianthe, yes, Metharme cried ;
But is it like young Hebe ? Were it not
That serving scarcely suits, it well might be
Her Mother awestruck at the bolts of Zeus.
    Myrrha thought gay Metharme just ; and
    said
Eos the tender were a fitter form
For Hebe : being active she could fill
For all the Gods, and ready be again

Ere the first bowl was drained.

                        The sprightly Neis
Declared Eos as Hebe would be waste :
No need for such a wondrous length of stride
Passing from God to God.   As Syrinx she
Were better far ; though, had the Nymph been
    fleet
As Eos, Pan had worn his clattering hoofs
To stumps before he caught her !

                        Eos thought
She might be fashioned Nymph of Artemis
To hurry thro' the woods with bow and spear.

  Eos, your thought is vain, Smyrna replied ;
Seeing an arrow-stricken stag throw long
Last filming gaze towards the fading hills,
Would wear with tears those great blue timid
    eyes
To redness like his wound.

                    Next Clytie thought ;
She would not yet say what she thought.   To
    her

The statue seemed more like Ianthe than
A statue.   Is it pardonable fault
For statue not to look one ?   She had doubts.
   Pygmalion's hand took Thisbe; him she
     thanked
With upraised eyes, head gently bending low.
   Euphrosyne thought Phœbe's judgment just ;
But felt with Clytie.   Never statue she
Had seen of man or God to her was worth
Such warm respect, so pleasant on the sight.
This was perchance most due to love she bore
Ianthe : for in truth the statue looked
Ianthe, but without her charm.   Though this,
Wanting her placid voice and ways, was more
Than art in fullest flower can fairly give.
What says Aglaia ?

               Meek Aglaia said
The features wanted rarer loveliness ;
An easier grace to sway throughout the form ;
A closer fineness in the lengths and joints
Of those grand limbs to be Ianthe.   Though,

These needful changes made, she should regard
The work as worthy to be named from her
Who underwent the burden and the toil
Day after day posturing motionless
Many exhausted moons.   Her charge, to hold
The household Gods inviolate, made her,
Perhaps, note statues more than others.   But
She from Calliope would like to learn
Her thoughts ; for, calm observer, often she
Sees more than those who talk.

                Thus challenged spoke
Calliope : she longed to make a change
In name.   Instead of Hebe serving Zeus,
Ianthe pouring for Pygmalion.
Of fit or unfit no complexities
Need then intrude to vex and mystify.
The statue telling its own simple tale,
Tho' from Olympus brought to common earth,
Yet faithful to its name, enchants all hearts
To love, by candour and simplicity.
  Then spoke the Matron. All have given theirs,

Now let us hear Ianthe's thoughts ; if she
Would like the statue named from Hebe, or
Herself.   But just, after Pygmalion's wish,
Her wishes should be first.

As all agreed,
They asked the Maiden frankly to declare.

Metharme then :

Ianthe ; hair is smooth,
Else look you, now, as on that blustering day
Returning from your wrestle with Boreas,
All apple-blossom.   When we had such dread !

Ready the titter.   Dainty shoulders rose
And shook ; some Maids took instant coughs,
        and some
Looked gravely wise, their hands before their
        mouths.

Pygmalion's Mother asked why on the cup
Young Eros sported with Euphrosyne ?

Ianthe, shy and all aglow, believed
Pygmalion only knew undoubtedly
His aim, and if his efforts struck or missed ;
The name must therefore rest with him alone.
She postured for him, as she daily poured,
When bringing food at noon ; in both she hoped
Aiding his toil : but neither gave her claim
To take from Hebe, an Olympian God,
Her name, and glorify herself therewith.

Abundant was Pygmalion's thankfulness,
Acknowledging the careful scrutiny
Of the whole noble throng ; he promise made
To weigh well every hint ; especially
Of tender Eos, for those lights she cast
On dark doubts in his soul.

                       Laughingly, she,
At speeches I am overmatched, but come
Down to the shore and test my speed to
       where
The lion-rock pushes his paws beneath

The waves: ten, your own paces, you shall take
Before I start.

               Nay Eos, you could give
Twelve, I believe, and then have better chance.
But know, O fleet One, some are made to
      stand
And fight, and some to run away.   But when
Some blessëd warrior calls our Eos his,
Not by rough capture will he win the prize:
That must be won by mild approach ; for she
Had beaten great Achilles unequipped
Though swifter than all Greeks.

                   With pretty praise
My Lord makes wonders of his Maiden's gift,
And hopes, by dazing us, to blink retreat
And show his skill in words.   But will he sing
With equal fortune if I challenge him
To contest for a song?

                Willingly he
Would try a verse: taking his lyre in hand,
With solemn countenance he struck the chords.

Darkly whisper forest leaves
>When I am sad ;
Brighter things they say to me
>When I am glad.
I would they laughed the gladsome things
>When I am sad ;
I should not hate those whispers dark
>When I am glad.

On bough a white dove gazed at me
>When I was sad ;
In grass a serpent gazed at me
>When I was glad :
I hated dove to gaze at me
>When I was sad ;
I laughed to see the serpent gaze
>When I was glad.

Then Eos taking her Lord's lute began

>Vaguely prattle forest leaves

When I. am weak and dreary ;
Mighty things they talk to me
When I am strong and cheery.
    O reverse them !

I feared a linnet's gaze at me
When I was weak and dreary ;
And scorned a serpent's gaze at me
When I was strong and cheery.
    Why rehearse them ?

A merry clash of laughter pealed around
As Eos ended.   Loud the verdict rang
The shortest being best ; though something like
The song before.   Pygmalion also laughed,
Avowing, gaily, that an audience pledged
To one against the other, could not hold
The balance true.   The Judges therefore he
Impeach'd of favour to the sacred Nine.

The   sentence   passed ;   the   Judgment   now
    broke up,

Leaving Pygmalion to his solitude.

His bitter longing still unsatisfied.

From noontide's broadest blaze no light for him:

From spacious clouds, the noontide's chariots,

Traversing day's eternal dome in long

White ranges splendid, or receding far

To ether pale, he saw no God descend.

When asked, the wandering winds gave no
    regard

Adventuring on to wastes remote, unknown.

The flowers kept fast their secrets why so bright

And bountiful of sweets.   Successive waves

Told only their own regularity,

Though ever whispering to the sands they kissed.

And men in council, or in market-place

Seemed unto him babbling of emptiness.

Hard unresponsive was the open world ;

No voice spoke cheer within.   At length re-
    solved

On craving aid from Heaven, to Her Temple he

With offerings of doves and myrtle boughs,
Wearied and anxious sought the Queen of Love.

Before a pan of fire on tripod placed
Pygmalion knelt.   All unabashed his doves
Cooed in their new-found home complacently.
The Priestess incense burned ; then throwing on
The myrtle boughs, with feathers chosen, she
Bade him look on the Goddess fronting him
With fixed regard ; neither to left nor right
Swerving, by gaze or glance ; above, below ;
Nor look behind ; but offer prayer and wait.

Departed then the Priestess ; leaving him
Alone with Aphrodite and the fire.

The flames and fumes between them : as he
    gazed
The Goddess seemed to tremble ; Her sweet
    smile
Wavering to sweeter meaning.   He felt faint

For joy ; hazarding an audacious hope
To hear Her voice responsive to his prayer.

O Goddess, Aphrodite ! Queen of All,
Thou knowest how I am thy loving slave ;
And how devoted to thy services
I have been since my memory's earliest dawn :
That beauty is to me the worth of life
Beauty thy privilege, thy very self.

When but a babe my nurse against her
    full,
Soft, youthful bosom fondled me to sleep.
My hands in never-ending play about
Her breasts travelled delightedly, till she
Kissed me to slumber and forgetfulness.
This, Goddess, was Thy worship.

                          Have not I
Ever been diligent for fateful glimpse
Of thee in graceful movement ; comeliness
Of features ; and the captivating forms

                    F

Throughout variety's extremest bounds
In women perfected, and tenderest maids!

When every creature of the living world
Breathed spring's redundancy, no heart has beat
More warmly true to Thine enamoured doves
In breezy pine tops, or on ground astrut,
Than mine.   Thy sparrows shrill in twittering
          flocks,
Tho' waging havoc on my promised fruits,
Have I alway protected in my love
For Thee.   Myrtles I planted, intermixed
Abundantly with roses, glowing praise
And prayer in blushing spaces odorous,
For worship of Thy love.
                              In ocean waves
Thy presence have I felt encompass me
When they have lashed my limbs to lustihood ;
Or on them I have lain in perilous sway
While wondering if the overhanging heaven
Were azure deep and lustrous as Thine eyes,

Whose emanations fill the strongest Gods

With tremblings like to mortals smit by fear,

Or eagerness for onset.

                 It is told

In ancient stories borne from man to man

That all the Gods love Hebe.   Zeus lets

    play

On Her His gentlest smile ; and pauses ere

He takes the nectar from Her offering hand.

When She is present Hera looks so sweet

Zeus scarce would honour fair mortality

With grace so freely did She thus remain.

Fierce Ares, He, raising the joyful bowl

Grins His delighted thanks.   Poseidon, when

He smooths caressingly Her lifted cheeks,

Declares, that saving Cytherea's self

Old ocean never owned so fair a flower.

And great Athena tones Her mighty voice,

Acknowledging that nectar tendered thus

Proves drinking wise, and wisdom beautiful.

And Hyperion's eyes such fire emit

That Hebe's dazzled eyelids fall as She
Fills, and ungazing holds the proffered bowl.

Striven have I, O Goddess, to create
Hebe's similitude as She might stand
Filling His cup for Zeus.   I made her young ;
Fair in her countenance ; well-shaped in limb ;
And lightly poised in force of mute reserve.
But spark divine, the throbbing touch of pulse,
To touch all other pulses as Her own,
She lacks, and looks as one who had not woke.

My utmost being done, having so failed
By mortal effort, I to Thee appeal
O Aphrodite, in Thy love of man
To yield the secret, that my handicraft
May truly show the awe my spirit feels :
Send from Olympus Life!

                              Pygmalion ceased.
His senses closed.   And from him parted then

His inmost self to meet the Goddess, now
Aloof and beaming in resplendent light,
And shedding azure radiance from Her eyes ;
She, brightly clad in tissue sunbeam-wove,
Diaphanous, no charm concealed whereon
He in his awe sublimely dared to gaze;
For, like the sun thro' wavering mists of morn,
Her beauty pierced.

            In rapturous suspense
Awaiting lips divine to speak his doom,
Conscious became he of ethereal sound
That filled the universe with song.   Each star
Joining the chorus in celestial praise
To her the Queen of life and loveliness ;
Whose voice came to him like a violet gust
From breezy earth in spring.

            Know you that I
Breathe in the lilies' perfume : daffodils
Awake surprise, taking their light from me.

I teach the tender nightingales my thought,
Rejoicingly they warble in the moon.
I start the thistledown's adventurous quest
For increase in some happy spot.   I nerve
Doves to such boldness hawks would they
        attack :
And lions soothe to gentleness so fond,
Harmless they sport as playful butterflies.
To spin like maids bent I strong Heracles,
And Zeus I tempted to become a swan !
I draw his clouds together ; make them fight ;
Embrace in flame, and breed live thunderbolts
For Him.   I put the edge on war.   To peace
I add the honey.

                    You have felt my power :
And shown due reverence by sacrifice,
Fitting obeisance, and observances
The negligent and savage disregard,
The burden borne attests the mortals' faith ;
And hissing flesh on altars rich men give

Often but vaunted unfelt offerings
Costing the giver not one cup of joy !
  The prayers and sacrifices loved of Gods
Are man's delight in giving up delights,
And checked impulses of the yielding will.
Your blameless life has been devotedness
To worship of my Beauty through your love.
You, wandering darkly, on a starless waste,
Tho' worn and sore from stumbling, have not
    paused
In faithfulness, and true to early bent
Have sought my succour in perplexity.
  This my reward, your Hebe shall have life
And immortality.   Far times to come
Shall sing your story.   Not the sweetest dream,
As stretched you lay on shadowed forest bank,
Has ever promised such a paradise
As mine awaiting you.

            But hark !   Before
These high Olympian gifts are yours to hold,

Braced must you be to battle for your own.

Dire hate will strew your path with scorpions,

And dog you for your life.   Foul calumny

Will taint your name with poisonous lies, truth-
     tinged,

Whereat familiar friends fall back appalled,

While other loved ones fledge the barbëd lies.

   For Gods do not their rarest gifts bestow

Without sure test and payment.   Men cannot,

In earthly state handle pure truth and fire,

The means of Gods, and still remain unscorched.

But you are strong ; the prize shines bright in
     view,

Cost what it may a pathway must be cleared.

And if you forward press unfalteringly,

Pallas Athena may beside you march.

   Now Cytherea's dulcet chanting ceased ;

And on his brow Pygmalion felt Her breath

Touch him like frost or fire, and knew no more.

BOOK V.

IN lonesome chamber, darkened, hushed, and
  cool,
Pygmalion lay asleep.   Beside him sat
His Mother watchful, listening every breath,
Timorous and awestruck at the strange event.

The   Priestess   found   Pygmalion   stretched
  before
The tripod where the fire was dead, and he
Himself seemed dead.   The Temple Guardians
  bore
Him home, and told all they could tell ; when
  she,
His Mother, soon by arts her son restored
To life, by chafing ; soothing cordials warm
And prosperously enticing grateful sleep.

Now she sat by and watched him slumbering.
No deadliest hate that vigilantly eyes
Its victim for the grievous chance, could watch
With keener vision than she scanned each
  change
In her belovëd son, the beautiful.

Her soul ran thro' the past ; when he a babe
Against her breast would pause to laugh, and
  leave
His food neglected : while the warlike sire
Smiling, declared her eyes would starve the child.

Well she remembered when she lost her Lord,
The dreadful numbness in her brain ; the pang
That clenched her heart ; and her Pygmalion lay
Sorrow be-dabbled in her helpless arms ;
She not unconscious in some time remote,
That sobbing form might grow a comforter
To shield her from mischance.

                        Anon she thought

With terror should Pygmalion pass away,
What would the world be then ?   No Hus-
 band's rule ;
No point of rally in the unmanned house :
A wheel without its tire.   Her thoughts sank
 low
And gathered darkness in the deepening,
While faintness crept within.

      Alarmed she saw
Pygmalion start and push the coverlet
Off his heroic shoulders and broad chest,
Asking if it were night ; and why she sat
Distraught beholding him ; and would she lift
Aside the curtain and let in the light ?

 She hastened and obeyed wonderingly :
Then told him of the Temple Guardians' Tale ;
His fall before the altar ; how they brought
Him to the house as he were dead ; how she
Had soothed him into sleep; from which she now
Thanked all the Gods of heaven he did awake
With senses perfect, full of questioning.

Have food for me dear Mother, I will take
A plunge into the waves, when you shall see
My appetite is sound whatever else
May halt; the rest must tarry now.

                                          She left
With trembling paces : her full gratitude
A feast triumphal rich with new delights.

    At eventide where they could hear the splash
And lisp of everlasting waves sat they,
Pygmalion and his Mother, underneath
An ancient olive where at hush the wind
Whispered of peacefulness for evermore.
    And there he told her of his sacrifice ;
How prayer made to the Goddess brought
    response
In Aphrodite's overwhelming grace.
Her promise of some mighty good, which
    though
Certain as fate not thereupon unveiled ;
Followed by threat of taint like pestilence ;

Friends become foes ; shrunk fear, or sudden
    death.
How horror of unwonted foul despite
Palsied his steadfastness : sank faint his heart,
When lo ! the Goddess neared and touched his
    brow
With breath of frost that entered like a spear,
And nothing knew he more.

                     She him assured
The Gods were just ; his faith must patiently
Await their issue.   Aphrodite's words
Would cheer him as a shout victorious
In effort's closest press.   Malignant hate ;
Backsliding friends, chorussed disdain ; the
    mince
Of small malevolence ; these take O Son
As tempests ; blight in corn ; raw chills of wind,
And earthquakes ; hard and burdensome to
    bear,
But in the course of things ofttimes irks more
Opposing than to loftily endure.

Decrees of Fate outspoken by the Gods,
What mortal dares gainsay?

                   When Egypt old,
Unglutted from her gorge of swallowed states,
Rapacious still, sailed with a fleet of war
On Cyprus to engulph us with the rest ;
The King and Rulers by a weight of votes
Assigned your Father the command in chief
To give their visit welcome. Slighting not
Old Egypt's power so dread and imminent,
He made disposal of the Island force,
No breathing time of loss. Piously then
To great Athena's Temple went and prayed
Whatever good the Gods would deign to grant,
Of aid and guidance to maintain the state
Against fierce Heathen who abhorred our
    Gods,
And would their fanes abolish ruthlessly.

He said that as a voice might sound in
    dreams,

These words came to his soul.   '

                        Await the foe
Fast by the landing-place in part concealed.
Your men rank close in shape of hollow wedge.
A trusted Leader place at either horn.
Yourself within the apex give command.
Move swiftly to and fro on either side.
Hold well aloof a strong force in reserve.
The foe when dashed, his every charge repulsed,
Signal your onset ; charge with all your strength.
The fairest death is death in victory,
Gods love the Brave who fighting for them die.

    His head was bent in reverence when the
        sound
Had ceased ; but conscious was he of some touch
That thrilled and ran throughout his brain like
        fire :
Whereon he rose, his purpose luminous,
His resolution fixed.

When leave he took
Of her, she said, more sweet his tenderness
Than in the earliest yearning flush of love.
Whatever might be his appointed fate
It would be hers to know her sweetness made
His life a blessing.   Should the blade of war
Cut short his thread, he bade her not bewail
As he should fall obedient to the Gods,
Man's highest privilege.   That she would find
The future of their Boy an ample world
For love ; forethought ; and fortitude to bear
Changes inevitably born of growth.
And should she grace him in her memory
As cenotaph he wished their Son be taught
His Father's deep immeasurable love.

Then in his arms he took her silently,
Both rapt in feelings that could not be told
While Time pulled in his rapid steeds and
          paused.
When low the sun flashed light in mighty beams

Clouding in glory the Olympian Gods

High placed for worshipping and household
    Guards,

The sigh he gave seemed drawn from Hades'
    depths

By one permitted for a task to breathe

Our upper world ; holding her head between

His hands, he kissed her brow and wetted eyes,

Then sharply turned away.

                              On either side

Without, the Maidens, servants, crowding slaves,

Ranged to behold him leave.   Each Maiden's
    hand

He lifting courteously kissed ; then bowed

His kingly head to all around and went.

She watched him up the rutted chariot way,

Till he had reached where Temple columns closed

The view : when, turning round his spear he
    raised

And twirled it in an airy circle, as

If greeting her with triumph ; thus, she hoped,

G

He went not sad at heart to meet his fate :
She knew he tried to make her think him glad.

When back were beaten Egypt's smirking
    hordes
In flight confused rushing to reach their ships ;
Pointing the chase, your Father, strides advanced
Beyond his warriors, neared so fast the shore,
Drew on himself a concentrated shower
Of arrows aimed to cover the retreat,
And, as the Oracle foreshadowed, fell.

They would not let me see his lifeless form,
So marred and mangled by the volleyed death.
But after rite and ceremony fit
All that was left of my own honoured Lord
A brazen vase contained : a pinch of dust,
Fragments of calcined bones, and memory.

The nation's victory was overcast
And saddened by their Chief's untimely close.

The King bewailed him as a dearest son
Who might awhile have shared his throne, and
    borne
Hereafter the whole burden.   Such the trust
His nature bred.

                Here sitting with your hands
In mine ; feeling their hard and massive size ;
And interlaced these boughs above our heads
Thro' whose selfsame intricacies we watched
Stars lighting their illimitable world,
I feel almost as if I yet held his.
But O my son, tho' you have been to me
More than your Father or myself could hope,
Not even you could fairly equal him.

    There was such reverence in his courtesy
Acceptance seemed conferring privilege,
So graciously he owned acknowledgment.
And all his kindly acts came in the course
Of nature ; not as efforts meant to please :
And gratitude awakened glad surprise
That life so teemed in blossoming delights.

His courage ; wisdom ; and his fortune he
Held but as trusts the state might call upon,
And not as private rights to sacrifice.
Therefore the King and Best exampled him
As worthy for their sons to imitate.

    You are, Pygmalion, flawed with moodiness ;
Strange spells of absence from the world, as
    though
You dreamed in daytime while the limbs per-
    form
Unerringly.   Sometimes I fear mayhap
Wanting a Father's firm control, who would
Nip freakish shoots and regulate increase,
Have left to wander wildly tendencies
That might have flourished to a kindlier crop.

    To hear my Father praised, and thus, by you
O dearest Mother, gives me sure foretaste
Of what the Oracle so surely told :
For never heretofore have I rejoiced
With such a full and bounding throb of pride

As now you tell of his heroic death,
Saving the state, commanded by the Gods,
Slain, but not conquered.　For such men as
　　he
Ride on the wings of Victory ; or they
Enter the gates of Death as Conquerors,
Invincible in life.
　　　　　　　In these strange moods
Sometimes I feel the Gods hold me in thrall
Disclosing laws larger than govern states.
Of truth's eternity : the accident
Of time ; the nothingness of space ; the force
Of pure resolve.　The fate of reckless ones
Who disregard their signs and oracles,
And omen pregnant with their wills sublime.

　My heart were pained, O mother, could I
　　think
In common paths my duty halted lame.
But dare I plod blind and unheedingly
When light immortal opens on my sight ?

The light of stars in his rapt lustrous eyes.
His tenderness ; even poor slaves his care
Protected often from deserved mishap.
The fire of strength, his resolution swift !

Thus mused the Matron ; hands still clasp-
    ing his,
Remembering his skill in warlike arts ;
Severe devotion to his godlike work ;
She owned, although strangely dissimilar
From her great Husband's constancy of worth,
Not less, but other was Pygmalion.

BOOK VI.

RELAX Orsines, your left arm relax :
In that which holds the spear I want your
  strength.
If this you tighten you draw force from that ;
And Dionysus meant a deadly wound
When pointing steel at grim Lycurgus King ;
Compel your strength where strength will best
  avail.

So spoke Pygmalion to his willing friend
Who stood as Dionysus.   Light his love
For sculptured forms and mimicry on walls ;
But as a graybeard with a favourite child
For love will join his pastimes and pursuits,
That otherwise were moil and weariness,.

Orsines loved to posture God or man
Aiding Pygmalion's service to the Gods.

Thus on they toiled thro' many a summer morn:
One's ardour warming to lay hold and show
That force the other did his best to give.
One day they argued on the people's press
For power, which turned against them to their
         bane
Unguided by the Best.   How wantonly
Their abject faith in mouthing demagogues
Noised empty phrases into oracles,
And gave base maxims vogue by utterance.

Orsines   thought   these   bubbles   might   be
    touched
By spear and sword with profit to the state.
To cut off thistles ere they flower and seed
Saved wasting soil and spared the labourer.

Nay, nay, Orsines, you a warrior trained

By daily exercise in warlike feats
Tend to resolve all tangles by the stroke
Of steel.   But steel, O friend, will scarce suppress
A rising tide ; or backward push the sun
Because forsooth his beams too fiercely burn !
Against the tide we must protect our shores
By driven piles ; and stones in sloping walls ;
And quays of solid strength.   Then tides become
The servants of our greatness, bearing ships
Exultingly to conquest ; or in peace
Enriching us by gathered merchandise.
We must not throw sharp sand against the wind.
No; we must strive to guide not stay this growth;
For tho' we are in our high state the flowers,
The people are the mighty stem whereon
We live and grow ; or perish if cut off.

Orsines thought Pygmalion must hit true
As, tho' in arms by far his overmatch,
He beat him worse in words and arguments ;
And meekly prudent ventured no reply.

Pygmalion asked what did Orsines think ;
Would lengthening our bows by one good span
Increase the force within the men's control ?

Orsines said the attempt were dangerous.
The men might hold the force well in command,
And aim as truly as at shorter range ;
But if attacking over greater space,
With sword and spear, their breath might fail before
The close, and profit thus the waiting foe.

Ianthe, radiant, entered while he spoke,
With wine ; and bread ; and fruit ; these plac-
        ing by
She said,

            May I pour wine for you my Lord
Orsines ?

            Rough and simple warrior he
Would take of wine, yea verily he would.

And as she offered him the well-filled cup
He reddened to the roots of his black curls
Vowing he fain would pour for her instead.

A strangely ordered Ganymede would you
Make my Orsines with your knotted beard
And hands of sinewy grip.   Old stories say
Hephaestus once poured nectar for the Gods,
And made Olympus with such laughter shake
The wrath of Zeus in thunder scarce had made
A greater uproar.   But of Ares yet
I have not heard he so amused their feast.

Orsines said that maids so often poured,
And tended on the wants of men, that men
Might change at times and tend upon the maids.

Ianthe looked amazed at words so sleek
From Chief so rough.   Pygmalion laughing cried
It is our Island's lack of war that tames
Orsines into peaceful courtesies.

Both gazed upon Ianthe as she moved
Across the chamber to the doorway where
Beyond the day was shining bright and still.
When, while her figure moved dark and defined
Against the outside glare, both inwardly
Felt there was something yet more fair than light.

Orsines told Pygmalion how alway
His Mother, older and in lassitude
Beyond Time's warrant, urged him constantly,
In mild pathetic plaint, that he would bring
Her home a daughter to her loneliness,
As she had never since my Father fell,
The day your own great Father met his fate,
Much mingled with the cheerful world without.
She yearns for children's laughter in the house ;
Her breast is dry for longing.   Pattering feet
Would be as music to her heart.   The clasp
Of tender little fingers ; kisses soft
That baby lips give sweetly, as the prankt
Delicious honeysuckle utters sweets

To every wandering zephyr that demands,
Her pent-up desolation would, she says,
Release in new-born joy of young delights,
And she again partake of blessed life.

How comes it my Orsines you so fail
Fulfilling her such reasonable hopes ?

It comes Pygmalion from the hindering fact
That though I have seen many noble maids
Too good and fair for my rude warrior ways,
Yet have I not seen one who strikes my soul
With sense of possibility that I
Could pass untired with her my lifelong course
Till now; when suddenly, as I saw her,
Ianthe, asking should she pour for me
I felt I could for ever with her dwell,
And she would be my home. Therefore, as
     you
Are Lord and Guardian of her fate, I ask
Permission to declare my suit, and take,

If graciously received, the Maiden home
To cheer my Mother with delightful hopes.

What ails Pygmalion ? You are deadly pale.
Your hand is on your heart !

                                    I know not what :
The heat, maybe ; but as you spoke there came
A dagger in my heart that cut in twain
Its very substance, so it seemed to me
For one brief momentary hell.   Tho' now
The pain is loosening slowly and I feel
Blood throbbing in my veins.   The Oracle
Of Aphrodite claimed full recompense
For some strange good to come, and now, per-
        chance
Payment begins in pain.
                                    This large request
Of yours somewhat astounds by suddenness.
My judgment must be calm and cool ; I must
Consult my Mother's will ; the Maiden's self

And her own wishes must be sacred held.

These must be known and weighed before I
    durst

Give even my Orsines promise fair,

Or aid to gain the splendid prize he craves.

The Maidens and my Mother are so bound

Together, that to pluck one from their midst

Will seem to them like pulling down their home

In wreck and ruin.   But ever on creeps Time,

Or stalks with giant strides.   Those cherished
    most

Leave us to shape their destinies, maybe

By us seen never more.   Or we leave them

Driven by passionless Necessity.

To-morrow ere the sun has set expect

Me at your house with message of your fate.

Lonely and sad Pygmalion left his work

To pace the solitary strand, where wave

Incessantly repeating wave soothed him

With movement in monotony.   The shriek

Of wild sea-fowl passing athwart the blue
Cried of some unborn sorrow yet to rise
And pierce his life with helpless agony.

How came it Gods made mortal future dark,
Unshielded, blind against the ills to come?
We know our aspirations : who can tell
If ever one will have the wings to fly
And reach attainment in the living day !

We grope, and dream of light, as moths are
heard
Tapping and scraping in the chrysalis
To gain the outer air.   And gained, what then ?

Came to Pygmalion's memory when a child
He heard a moth scrape at his prison-walls
With energy unflagging.   Worn, at length
The side began to tremble to and fro,
Scarcely a film, which the small creature burst
And struggling out, all moist and crumpled,
clung
To his sometime tomb.   Motionless awhile

The warm air dried his wings, to gorgeous hues
Expanded : these for a time he fluttered,
Then half an arm's length rose, and wavered
    back.
This did he thrice, then paused. Last, gallantly,
In power complete and noble sweep uprose ;
But reached not more than half the tree's height
    ere   .
A darting bird from out the branches seized,
And gorged him in mid air.   This pirate, too,
Had ears and eyes in watching for his prey,
Whose first flight from his dusky prison-house
Was to his grave in that rapacious maw.

H

BOOK VII.

Breathe, O breathe, ye perfumed lilies,
Worshipping great Aphrodite!
Shout and sing, O nightingales,
Giving voice to Aphrodite!
Her's the power that binds his breath
When the lover's accents fail!

Thus chanted troop of girls at morningtide,
As towards the Temple they, with roses piled
On baskets, went to worship Cytherea
In loosely ordered march.   Some on their heads;
At arms' length some; and some resting on hips
Their baskets bore; while other loads so large
Took two young girls to carry one between.

In strange perplexity Pygmalion heard

The chanting girls, as he was passing near.
The chant seemed but the echoed Oracle ;
And he, bewildered, wondered if in dreams
The sound had mixed ; or had divinely come
From Aphrodite as the voice of Fate.
Would ever Hebe bring the fire from heaven ?
Should he the Treasure find, and foul despite
Crawl withering on his track like pestilence ?
But after much vain thought and wandering,
Seeing by shadows' fall and city signs
It lacked but one good easy hour of noon,
He loitered homeward on Orsines' suit.

   True to her time Ianthe entering
Saw Lord Pygmalion not at work ; instead,
Pacing with silent footfall to and fro
The spacious floor.   She placed the food and
        wine,
And moved towards the doorway, when he called
Bidding her stay;

                I, maiden, must perform

A task, a duty; right it may be called.
I want your keenest ear ; it may be fate.

He was abrupt; his words were harsh; no ring,
Or gentle intonation in his voice.

Ianthe felt a dull cloud on her soul
That shadowed her without significance,
And stood in silence waiting.
                                                    He began,
Orsines tells me that he loves you well,
And ask'd my aid to make his wishes known.
His Mother wants a daughter, he a wife,
And you, he hopes, may fill the wants of both.
My promise was that I would lay his wish
Before you and my Mother ; you to choose.
What say you, Maiden ?
                                                    I wish not to wed.

Orsines is of birth high as your own.
Before our Island merged its petty Kings

In one great Kingship, reigned his ancestors,
Ruling a vast and fertile stretch of land.

Birth would not tempt a Maid.   And lineage
    high
Maidens of lineage take by right, as they
Take food and air ; but not as privilege.

But my Orsines, he is brave beyond
Most men.   He blithely would give play to three
And beat them off with loss.

Brave men are brave
In nature's course, not brave for us alone.
A bull mightily guarding cows in mead,
Show him another bull, or garment red,
And judge if he is scant of bravery.
Loose on him leash of dogs from Ithaca,
Behold if they that quality will lack !
Once when your Father watched his woodmen
    fell
A blasted oak that sucked up nourishment

And darkened out the sun from ripening vines;
Was heard a crash, a torrent-roaring rush,
From which a monstrous boar, aflame with eyes
And gleaming tusks, and bristling horrent light,
Made towards them down the slope.   Swift as
        a bird's
Wingbeat, your Father fronted him and poised,
While, as the horror furiously charged,
He, swerving, just escaped with graze on hip ;
Then with a woodman's axe, in both hands
        clenched,
He stood astride awaiting the return.
But when the baffled monster checked his course
And raging plunged to make the charge again,
Your Father, with unerring mighty stroke,
Drove in the blade between his fiery eyes
And slew him with one blow.
                                Such bravery
The man exalts : prompt adjunct to his will ;
His sacrifice ; and readiness to foil
The possibilities of dark mischance !

Maiden, your thoughts are wise and truly spoke;
And he, Orsines, mates those lofty words.
　　Young maidens must not flinch; they owe
　　　　the state
Some service; wed they must to rear up sons
For work and war, and daughters to delight.

　　A Maiden does not cast so far before,
And such concernings leaves in Hera's charge.
Hurt am I Lord, in being followed close
From point to point by chasing arguments;
Thus made to turn and double like a hare
Before remorseless hounds, to save myself.

　　Pygmalion was appalled.
　　　　　　　　　　　　Ianthe hurt!
That were indeed disgrace and wrong,
　　　　he sighed.

Gazing he looked so woebegone, so lost,
The Maiden's soul was smitten: mournfully

She spoke;

Pardon, my Lord ; I would not wound
You in return because you wounded me.
But Maidens are not made to love against
Their natures.   Arguments can never change
A hawk to meekness, or inspire the dove
With lust of rapine on the feathered race.
  I have no thoughts of wedlock.   When I wed
My love must come as worship ; not for one
Whose character and worth may be defined
And read like any act of daily life.
  Divinest sympathies are pre-ordained
By some eternal Power we wot not of ;
And should we violate their sanctity
We sink to lower state : our happiness
Curdles to self-contempt, and we are slaves.
Unversed am I in loves and marriages,
Having no Mother, Brother, Sister, Sire,
And knowing only your own Mother's love,
And love of all her Maids.

This know I sure,

The man who wins a noble Maiden's soul

Must noble be himself.   Suffices not

The dexterous use of bow and threatening
    spear ;

Nor staunchest loyalty to King and friends ;

My hero makes the region he commands

The richer for his life, and dying leaves

Open the path of his adventurous feet.

For Godlike effort thus alone marks man

From beasts, that eat their way thro' age to age

Unvarying, each like each.   Regard your own

High, difficult, and stern, laborious art.

What was it in the olden time when Greeks

Content with blindly imitating forms,

Limb-bound, and lifeless, of Egyptian Gods,

For generations made˗no step beyond,

Till Daedalus with new Promethean fire,

Carving the stubborn blocks of wood and stone

To limbs detached, gave to his images

The air of will and motion !   Rude, uncouth

They were.   But they had life, the breath of Gods!
And to be truly man a man must be
As Gods ; to make, and to create, and live
At one with nature.   Happy he whose soul
Aspires to dwell in that eternal calm
Where knowledge sees confirmed results ere yet
The fashioning hands have touched.   His life
        becomes
Akin with higher Powers ; his spirit fit
To stand before His throne and gaze on Zeus.

        Ianthe !
                O Ianthe !
                                Treasure found !
My Goddess !   O my Dearest !   Thou art She !

        Then at her feet he fell.   She bending
        clasped
His head close to her heart, as it had been
A tender little babe : gazing abroad
In terror mute.

And when he spoke
So strange the sound he knew not his own voice ;
And felt removed into another world,
As he some other was.

      Soon rising, he
Took her two hands and stood removed the
  length
Of both their arms ; and on her countenance
Now wet with tears, stared hard in wonderment.

Then lifting up his heart, that until now
Had been a weight of pain, he spoke to her:

How have I been, O loved Ianthe, blind !
The longed-for ripe perfection of my life
Here manifest before me day by day
Between the dawning and the setting sun !
And I from circumstance, not wilfulness,
O well may you believe, have seen it not !
But having found the Resting-place of this
My anxious self I will not wander more.

My Hebe, my most loved One ; I beheld
Now, when you saw Olympian Zeus enthroned,
And happy spirit gazing on His power,
Again the look divine I saw before,
And dreaded was the fragment of a dream
I never more might see !

                    Do you in truth,
In very truth, your Maid Ianthe love ?
And do you feel that she can give you joy
Thro' lifelong changes to gray fall of age ?
Or is it your wild rapture at some grace
Discerned in me that may advance your work
Makes you thus utter such bewildering words ?

Ianthe ; should the Gods of heaven combine
And offer make me of an added charm
For you, in stature, strength, or loveliness,
Or some sweet witchery I know not of,
So much I love you I should ask the Gods
To leave you perfect as I see you now.

The Maiden cried, Now my Pygmalion, I
Know that you love me !

                As she spoke she fell
Like a spent fountain at Pygmalion's feet.

   Sweetness and tenderness the words he
     spoke
To her held lifted in his powerful arms,
And as he bent to kiss her drooping mouth
He saw the glow of one white pouting breast
Rose pointed, proud, with glimmering azure
     laced,
Too fair for touch or even mortal glance,
   While holding her within his arms he sighed
And whispered low love's immemorial tale,
To her attention tranced ; he saw the pure
Pale countenance deepen in colour till
Her beauty glowed a rose in perfect flower ;
And splendour like a garment covered her.
Now burnt the dark gray eyes of dawn in full
Meridian glory :   Lustrous flashes flew,

And pierced his heart throbbing tumultuously
Like a thing captive by the hunter struck.

Herself releasing softly from his hold
She went and stood upon the platform where
So often she had postured for her Lord,
And, no way conscious, she the attitude
Of Hebe took, asked should the statue be
Smitten to life; should Athens, and should
    all
Proclaim him the first Maker of the world,
At such a time would he not feel it rash
To have her taken for his wedded wife
Ere his pride knew the swell of victory?

Ianthe, I have faith in Aphrodite.
The Treasure have I found; the Life will come.
Light effort now carving the lines that fire
The marble into passion, brand the thought;
I see them now clear and determinate.
You hold the fire; I see the glory burn!

Should every State of Greece, with Athens
    proud
To head them, crown me King of our whole
    race :
Should all the Gods in conclave ratify,
And after make me an Olympian God,
No other would I love, none take but you.

Now to my Mother; I will tell her Fate
Has crowned me with the diadem of joy.

His left around her waist, his right hand held
Both hers ; they proudly thro' the doorway went
Along the curving path : their stately forms
More seeming demigods than man and maid
On this our common earth.   They overpassed
Where once she saw within the doorway shade
The Lord Pygmalion stand regarding her.

The memory of that delightfulness ;
That unfamiliar music in her heart ;

Again she lost her feet, and saw herself
In bygone solitude with Echo nymph,
With Dido, Ariadne, and Medea.

   When they had reached the chamber where
        the Maids
At various tasks around the Matron toiled,
Pygmalion cried aloud,
                        O mother, I
Have found her!   Hebe She is come to life!

   The Matron and the noble throng as one
Cried in amaze
                    Your Hebe come to life!

   The palace slaves and servants standing by
Cried in amaze
                    His Hebe come to life!

Forgetful of respect some left in haste
With arms high-spread proclaimed the wonderful.

The city loiterers alway agape
For new births, shaped, or shapeless, as may be,
Rehearsed the cry, till some declared they saw,
Or knew some who had seen, in clouds of fire,
The Goddess Aphrodite pass into
Pygmalion's chamber.   But what there took
        place
None but himself and the dread Goddess knew.
But certain was it that the Statue walked
Straightway from his workchamber to the house,
Pygmalion's arms bound fast about her waist:
For all the noble Maidens saw ; and saw
The servants and the palace slaves, and cried
All with one voice
                Your Hebe come to life !

Also for certain the great Matron cried,
O Hebe ! O Ianthe !   Am I mad !.
And fell down in their arms, and likely dead.

I

BOOK VIII.

THE disk of Hyperion barely stands
At span above the ocean line ; I must
Haste to Orsines and report his fate.

In calm Ianthe's charge Pygmalion left
His Mother resting.   She had been distraught
In her amazement when Pygmalion came
Godlike and beaming with Ianthe, red
In newborn radiant love, crying aloud
Hebe had come to life !   And all as one,
Repeated Hebe, She is come to life !
Amazement fled in joyfulness, when she
Knew that Pygmalion and Ianthe loved,
And suddenness closed sense with its excess.
Soon came the light back to her happy eyes ;

The blood again soon pulsed in pleasantness,
Under the Maidens' and Ianthe's care.

Hail, hail, Pygmalion! You are light of
step.
The firm exactness of your tread speaks power
That would us mortals hold at high command!

Say not so, my Orsines. Sad the tale
For you I have to tell. Ianthe loves
Not you but me. Instead of gift divine,
Fiat of loss I bring, and baulked desire.

Look not so dolorous, Pygmalion.
The loves of maidens are like scents of flowers,
In giving forth their sweetness each complete.
If the tall lily scorn to gathered be,
The drooping jessamine perchance may shower
Her stars upon me bright and odorous.
Stain not that lovely face with tears. Believe
Me when I say more proud am I that thou

Pygmalion, Maker of great Gods ; strong Lord
Of bow, and spear ; warcraft, and ancient lore,
Shouldst make the peerless One, Ianthe, Wife,
Than had she willing come unto these arms.

    To whisper in your friendly ear, I was
Half frightened of success.   I feared that she
Were far too strong for my poor hands to hold,
And winged for regions I could never make.

    Noble Orsines, from my heart you ease
A pain I feel had wrung your own to know.
Some other where and when, not now, I will
In parcel tell how I my Treasure found.
But O my well-loved brother, I am grieved
That joy like mine should not be joy of yours,
And that for you there is no Resting-place.

    I hold it savours of discourtesy
To shoot conjecture through a maid's reserve ;
As though her secrets were but things of chase,
Untended, game for any venturous shaft.

But what to wantonness devoid of weight
Should be forbidden, to the Guardian lies
An open path ; not only charged with right
Of entrance, but with need to act and serve
Her, who perforce, must helpless be herself.

You know I love my Mother's noble Maids
Each one and all as they my sisters were :
But one so tender, and so young, so meek
In her wild timid ways, mayhap I love
Above the rest ; and she I think loves you.

The visage of Orsines now turned pale ;
And eagerly he forward bent to hear.

Eos the tender, we the Maiden call,
Of great blue timid eyes.

                              Pygmalion !   Say
You do not fool me with these precious words !
O Eos, loved One !   O my Soul on Earth !

Long, long ago, my dearest Heaven-sent
   friend,
I thought I loved young Eos.   Ever shy
She seemed of my rough presence ; in the house,
Or in the myrtle walks, and Temple Feasts.
I felt but a shagged mountain bear that strove
To woo a great-eyed fawn, or shining swan.
Resolved I would not fright, or be her bane,
I closed my heart against her once for all.
Till now I have not swervèd from my resolve,
Thinking my ancient interest in her dead :
But now !   O now !   And may I hope to win?

Orsines, you will win.   But hearken first :
I almost grudge that even Orsines should
Command the tender Eos.   Few who live
Can know in her the depth of tenderness !
So daintily attuned, that instrument
Responds in music to the faintest breeze ;
.While harshness would distract the chords and
   make

A jangle of her nature.   Gentle be
Your touch of her Orsines !   Low and soft
Your voice and words ; your meaning ever kind.
Then in your household will be light and
    flowers,
And a sweet bird singing throughout the day.

Orsines' head sank in Pygmalion's neck,
Long there he wept for very, very love.

Now with a certainty untroubled wrought
Pygmalion on his Hebe.   Great his joy
To raise the wonder in her brows.   To make
The shadows dark within her upward eyes :
In those fine nostrils breathing purity.
Pressing the mouth to longer droop of curves
Above the prow of her imperial chin.
These now in his fierce energy were but
As trifles.   Chisel edge could scarcely touch
Ere the obstruction vanished as a cloud.
    Yea, yea, he cried, the bowl divine should be

More firmly pressed ; for risk there must be
    none
Of waste in shaking the Olympian cup !
More tightly bound the joints; the dimpling be
Less spacious and more softly widened forth.

Aglaia, she was right ; throughout the lengths
Of the grand limbs perfection closer yet
Must I effect ere they afford the grace
Of Hebe or Ianthe.   The long sway
Will suavely come in lightening her waist
Both on the outward curve and inner line.

This knee !   In fineness dare I venture more ?
The heartshape of the cap: ah! just a shade! .

Yes !   Even a daughter and a Goddess feels
Something of tremulous in face of Zeus ;
Therefore this foot more pressure must admit,
As witnessing ethereal power that warms
And animates the whole immortal form
Of God obedient to the Thunderer's will.

Pygmalion's statue was completed, and
Crito, his own and Father's ancient friend

Came to demand the statue might be shown
Unasked for to the people as a boon.

Pygmalion cared not, he indifferent was.

Ianthe, who with Crito entered, said
Nowise indifferent, my Lord, art thou.
The matter has not fairly caught thy mind
And claimed attention due.   Thyself hast said
That men who do not show their works when
    done
Are either conscious of their worthlessness,
Or treat with traitorous scorn their fellow men.
For they assuredly stand traitors stark,
Refusing thus their miserable best
To their nativity and kindred race.

Lofty Ianthe!   Crito cried ; entranced
Am I to hear you strike heroic chord.
Our noblest dames too often hold their part
Enough to safely move on footworn ways,

Curbing adventurous sally in their Lords.
Not thus, Pygmalion knows, is our great world
Made greater.   Not by smiling effort down ;
Or wailing when her Lord takes spear and shield
To slaughter lions, boars, and savage beasts
That rage and ravage to the herdsmen's loss,
Wasting the country's wealth ; or meets his foes
To save her lovely self from slavery.

  True words are thine, Lord Crito! I have heard
Pygmalion ask what rank would ours be now
Had Orpheus never sung his songs divine.
  For he, King of the living Lyre, and Song,
Opened with music our astonished sight :
He put amazement in our souls to know
The life in rocks ; the spirit in each tree ;
The sweetness in the flowers themselves enjoyed.
He made the waters bound in frolic mirth,
Or calmly flow contentedly to sea :
The storm-entangled forests lash their limbs
And roar in stern triumphant harmony.

We are awake ; we are no longer dead !
Taught us, confiding brutes we kill to eat,
Own gratefully the strokes of gentleness.
That when the wild birds peck from infant hands
Affection more than want entices them.
. He sung that man slaying his brother man
To sate the bite of individual wrath
Was murder ; and for others' safety he
Who slays is banished, or tastes death himself.
Men were but brutes until Prometheus gave
Them fire from heaven.   But when they metals
        used,
And baked their corn, and made their dwellings
        firm ;
How were they more than brutes save in the
        strength
Of hardened points, and many bound as one ;
Till Orpheus sung them into sympathy
With forest flowers and lisping forest leaves :
With following creatures, that as helpful lords
Regarded men who reared them for their use ?

Fitting it was the nightingale should sing
Above his grave who sang so sweetly here.
Who sang wild man to worshipping the Gods,
The dread of Hades, and the pangs of crime!

Pygmalion said there was no longer doubt
The statue must be shown, but when and where?
He would not have an ever babbling stream
Disturb his working hours throughout the day.
What says our Crito, wisest Cyprian Lord?

Your chambers then are closed against the
      crowd.
Meseems Ianthe has first privilege:
The statue is of her, whose judgment sound
Will sift the circumstance and find the place.

Ianthe challenged thus pronounced its doom.

As I was the unconscious cause my Lord
Began the Statue: and as day by day

I gave him my best aid in posturing :
And when we had our best done that he failed;
And that responsive to his pious prayer
The Goddess Aphrodite promised gift
Of life ; that, not till then, could he make clear
The vision in his soul ; it seems to me
My Lord's relation and my own the same.
Nor he nor I have in the statue right
But as the ministers of higher Power.
And therefore I, Ianthe, now pronounce
The Statue be with ceremony fit
A sacred offering to the Goddess made, ·
And placed within her Temple for all time !

O blessed Ianthe my soul goes with thine !
Pygmalion cried ;

and Crito, pleased his word
Had borne a perfect blossom sweet to each,
With utmost reverence he dared believe
That Aphrodite through Ianthe spoke.

BOOK IX.

DREAMS are not always dreams as understood.
Fore-runners often they : first strivings dim
To handle things yet formless, or unknown.
While thus our souls full on adventure bound
Wing to encompass untried regions, new ;
Encountering Fiends opposed ; or graciously
Led by sweet Spirits safe to golden heights ;
Our bodies lie as fast asleep, or dead.
But not the will, that beats at strongest flight !
You did not dream Pygmalion : your soul heard
The song of Nature sung ; the kindling truths
Told by the Goddess.   We are instruments
Selected to convey the Gods' behests,
They play us as they please.

This Crito told

Pygmalion as they with Orsines marched
Processional, to offer thanksgiving
To Aphrodite for her mercies shown :
The newborn life ; the love She had vouchsafed;
And in Her Temple had his work allowed.

   The Matron Mother next ; on either side
Were Eos and Ianthe.   Paired, the rest
Of noble Maidens came.   Them following
A host of palace servants, each of whom
Held myrtle sprig or the red rose in hand.
Brightening each side the march a line of
    girls
Kept paces with them, chanting songs of praise
To Her, their Queen of love and loveliness.
Flanking the Temple steps, behind the Priests
And Temple Guardians, stood in double lines
A hundred warriors on each side ; their spears
And burnished shields two living streams of
    light
That awed the dazzled multitude, agape
With admiration.   Far beyond these lines

Were seen the crowds ; their heads astir they
    looked
Like plains of ragged growth moved by the
    wind ;
But noiseless, save for buzz and murmuring hum,
Expecting some deep mystery disclosed.
    When all the Temple entered, to the last
Whose claims the Priests allowed, and doors
    were closed,
Bursting the noontide silence rose a cry
Whose shivering echoes struck the city walls,
Startling far women at their spinning wheels
With wonder if an earthquake were afoot !
While sucklings dropt their mothers' breasts to
    cry.

 .Hail Lord Pygmalion whom our Goddess loves,
And brought for love his statue into life !
Hail to the Matron and her noble Maids !
And hail ye Warriors who do honour him !
And hail again, to Aphrodite, Hail !

Thus the great populace approval voiced,
Proud that Pygmalion's triumph was their own.

When in the sacred walls had been performed
Each ceremony and observance due
The march went homeward.
                              Now broke up the crowd
As stirred their various wills.   Their daily tasks
Hurried some off at speed.   While others
       lounged
At ease on Temple steps and drank the sun.
Mostly they clung in groups.   Rank and
       bemired
Some idlers from warm wallowing indolence,
By fits and starts grunted of this or that.
Pleased to vent ignorance of things august,
Some discussed hotly ; others prophesied
That henceforth statues all would come to life !
Was this a prodigy for once and all ?
If made to live would price of statues rise ?
What all would come to Gods alone could say !
                       K

Garrulous, and by smug listeners girt, there
　　sat
One of the dark deposits seething vice
Precipitates from scum in swarming towns.
A shape most like a blasted trunk, whose
　　limbs
Are withered boughs: the only brute life
　　shown
One yellow tooth, and two red glittering eyes.
She, unto one, a citizen, his bulk
Far wider round by measure than his height ;
His jowl from chin hung larger than his cheeks :
Small nose and eyes and wide capacious mouth.

Aye, aye, the Best ; we know what means
　　the Best.
Eating best meat ; drinking best drink ; best
　　clothes
To spoil ; the best made by hardworking
　　hands !
This is the Best they wot of.　In what else .

The Best, it passes me to know ; and I
Have age upon me and I ought to know !

    At this protested blandly, he so round.
They have their merits, as of course defects ;
They buy of us and we sound profits make.
Let us not quarrel with our meals ; but eat
All we can get, then look about for more.
No, no, the Best I cannot wholly hate.

    The fell tree-trunk declared that hate to her
Was what she breathed : she hated all the Best.
Look at this Lord Pygmalion ! Was he oaf,
Or sleek time-server ?   He, the Temple, that
Could well afford to buy, his statue gave :
Spoiling the statue market, these rich Lords !
Who ever knew the Priests to buy if they
Could sate their wants without ?
                              Was it to hush
The crime ?   For all know what he did.   Ha !
    Ha !

Prayed Aphrodite give his statue life!
The life he gave was blood.   He stabbed the
    maid
Who loved him : and he mixed her blood with
    clay,
And with that clay he made his statue live.
    Prayed Aphrodite!   Aphrodite knows
More natural ways of making shapely maids
Than killing maids to mix their blood with clay.

    Roundness remarked it was not well to rail
Too boldly at the Best : scoffs might by chance
Bounce to their ears : they might think well to
    shift
Their purchases and other purses fill ;
A change too horrible !   Let well alone ;
Let well alone say I ; for thrive I do
And grow the bigger for it as you see.
Look at Pygmalion and Orsines ; large
Most true, and tall ; but bones compared with
    me !

With that, self-satisfied, his Roundness
   swagged
From side to side, like vessel over-poised,
Cargo too heavy and too scant of keel,
And swaggirfg swayed himself lost in the crowd.

Meanwhile the vulture in that blasted trunk
Clutching thin air her scorching hatred barked.

Behold young Bacis, my own daughter's son.
She was well shapen till one of these Best
Fathered her boy : like Ariadne then
She took drink comfort in our island wine,
And grew bloat, dull, and purple. He, the
   Best,
Gave us the gold King-likenesses we loved.
But when cursed steel let out his life in war
Our fountain dried : we did the best we could.
She did her best ; but bloat and purple red
Draw young men less than whiteness, strength,
   and shape.

Discomfited with failure, more she drank ;
Swelled larger daily; caught the plague, and
    died.

    Young Bacis left, my withered shoulders bore
The luckless load.   Bright as a fox that boy.
Fox his sharp features ; fox his peering ways.
Many good meals he brought me, tho' where got,
Like a true fox my foxey would not tell.
He would have grown a lion would that fox,
For get he would, somehow ; would get and
    save ;
When having saved and scraped a heap of
    wealth,
What is he but a lion among men !
    This sneak ; this sleek Pygmalion what did
    he ?
He took him from his gutter playfellows ;
Sent him straightway to school : there had him
    taught
The statue-making, as he had a gift,

They called it !

         Foxey sharpness, with the eyes
To see what safely may be snatched, a gift !
Blind, blind these Best ; as blind as we are
    bright.

 Shame, shame, the listening Chorus cried, to
    take
Him from his gutter playfellows to school !
To make a statue-maker of a boy
Who might have saved and scraped a heap of
    wealth !

Inspired by choral sympathy, the fowl,
The dry gray fowl barked more from blasted
    tree.

And when my fox's sharpness learned the
    art,
Outstripping all the elders ; what was done
By this my Lord Pygmalion called of Best !

Much wanted he, the boy, to make a strip,
A narrow strip of wall, with figures cut
Thin, flat, and laid along its utmost length.
No toil could ever make him lag fatigued.
Sheepskins he took, scoured bright and clean ;
   these stretched
He tight and firm on frames, then drew the
   forms
Of men and maidens going to sacrifice
On horses, in proud chariots, and on foot.
In one part was a Fury marked ; the fox
Made my face into hers!   This world! this world!

This plan was shown the Priests.   A word
   from him,
Pygmalion, would have given my boy the work.
But did he give that word ?   I tell you, No !
Lip-gnawing jealousy, cold rankling there,
Would not allow a spawn of gutter drab
To brave it with the Best.
               Panting, she paused.

Shame, shame it was, the Chorus cried, to stop
The spawn of gutter drab from beating Best!

Then! what did Bacis do? He sank adown
From greatness he had never reached, because
That jealous Titan blocked his proper path.
O gold and purple that he might have won!
O brazen chariot, and O sweetest wines!
O maiden with the wealth he might have wed!
And now what does he do? Makes little gods
For dwelling-houses where the pay is small.
So I, instead of wearing linen fine,
Bordered with flowers in hue and threads of
    gold;
And having slaves to watch my every wish,
Must spin and drudge; or beg and steal and
    drudge.

Thus midden-heated, hatched the festering lies
That bred in multiplying swarms, and wove
A cloud of hatred round Pygmalion's name.

Some fat and full-blown, dashed with strains of
  truth,
Catching to careless glance, and shallowness.
Some crawled the dust intent ; by wriggling hard
Fixed themselves tight in unexpecting ears.
Others winged-born, and swift, in hovering buzz
Sought places from the rubs of life worn bare
To strike their pitiless and poisonous stings.

  Pygmalion, who unwitting this dark web,
Fine-meshed, far-reaching, was around him
      wrought,
Began to wonder friends he loved right well
Seemed shy or cold, or made abrupt replies
To common questionings of daily life.
Still passed them lightly by for fancies bred
Of over-charged endurance, such as his.
Had lately been.
            But when recurrence made
An evil meaning hideously bare,
He could no longer doubt an origin

For this estranged affection.　Clear survey
Then taking of past years and latter days,
He saw no conscious act or circumstance
In which he had been part could fairly raise
A coarse antagonism edging on
Malevolence.　Distrust but once aroused,
The lightning from a cloud no swifter went,
Nor straighter, nor more certainly than he
To his determined aim, now fixed to track
The mischief to the midden whence it sprung.

BOOK X.

WELL timed, Pygmalion, is your coming here !
I wanted some clear judgment on this shield.
First note the size is larger than prevails ;
Centre more raised, while smoothly at the rim
Returning forward in a gentle curve.
　　Now, you will ask, O Crito, why this change ?
And my reply is what these eyes have seen.
In many a stubborn contest ; arrows sharp,
And mightily thrown spears, have glinted off
And struck the men behind, sometimes to death.
Whereas this curve would check the shafts so
　　　　they
Fell harmless, or at worst would swerve length-
　　　　wise
And strike those near; but blow from staff of ash

Is unlike prick of steel.

                              Fair on its face
Your new device, and fair the arguments :
But why allow so many seasons pass
Ere you, O Crito, brought your shield to proof?

    My reasons are but these.   In battle's crash
We scarcely heed a thousand things we see,
So grimly set on holding to our lives,
And taking those opposed.   The fighting done,
The other thousand things we have to do
Leave scanty time for memories.   At length,
When order reassumes authority,
And we ourselves can give to our affairs,
Instead of wandering in the past, we find
The present swallows up our energies
Healing the gaps in fortune ; or by use
Of fortune's favours we have gained by war.
    But when a man is old, and knows his time
Now short among his fellows, comes to him
Desire to do some service ere he die.

And in this sunset of my life old friends
In arms, dim shades of ancient long-ago,
Come thronging, faces pale, regarding me ;
And one slain by a spear glanced from my
    shield
Brought this device to mind.   And now I hope
This may save others in the years to come.
    But stay : Pygmalion does not look himself :
Your eyes move restlessly ; your face is pale :
Safe the great Matron's and Ianthe's health ?

At those loved names a ray of pleasantness
Lighted his countenance as he replied :

Of pure and perfect health as birds in song
But I am somewhat troubled by cold smiles,
Or no smiles, and coarse scowls instead ; but why
And wherefore nought can tell.   Friends I
    thought kind,
Who hitherto responded graciously
To courtesies of mine, now darkly smirk ;

Or mince the countenance to acrid stare ;

Or standing by forget Pygmalion lives.

Another passing drops his face on breast

Plunged in profoundest thought ; whose thought
    erewhile

Had never risen beyond his sandal strings.

And twos will talk of things above my head

As if too high for me to understand.

Or if I question some give half replies

And start away on sudden business bound.

Others in laughing converse, when I near,

Cease, and compose their masks to unconcern.

While much of this I have for long observed,

And passed it by as fancy, or as chance ;

But now at length I know there must be root

And widely spread to grow such evil fruit

Of rudeness, spite, and hate, so come to you,

My wisest and most ancient friend, for help

To dig this mandrake from its hold and
    find

The planter, and to what his purpose trends.

Pygmalion, no hot-brained witling you !
Quick of offence, and ready to resent :
But calm and equable in intercourse ;
Less willing to reprove than take reproof :
And gentle often when you might be stern
With reasonable profit to your state :
Therefore, maintaining justice of your plaint,
I know some mischief-workers must have
　　　sown
What bear these Protean discourtesies.

　　Some rumours have I heard the statue men
Are disconcerted by unseemly fears
Their markets may be broken up and closed
Should this new art of making statues live
Kindle the people to demand of them
Like statues they would dread to undertake.

　　These rumours until now I flouted off
As meaningless ; vagaries ever rife
When any new thing fires the populace.
My business now I make to search and probe
This ulcer ; nor will stop till I release

The aggregated mischief; or discern
Its nature and its cause immediate.

   I have a sister's son, an orphan now;
No vice has he, but skittish as a colt;
And, save in things of weight, heeds me no
     whit,
In statue matters more especially.
He drifted in and joined a knot of youths
Fierce in archaic quaint proclivities;
Brazen of speech, and truculent in stare
On those infatuate, blind to Iris wings
In dusty darkness; in hoar ignorance
The wisdom and the wit! And age with them
Must be far back indeed; for Daedalus
They hold is far too free; his statues have
Too much of motion for archaic truth;
The only truth select ones care to know.

   Of this same sportive youth I will command
He sift archaic friends, and make research
To learn what this base comedy may mean.

L

To-morrow, the next day, or after that,
Should I not strike the vein before, I will
Disturb Pygmalion at his God-making
And open scroll of what I may collect.

    Farewell, dear Crito ; with those calm clear
        eyes,
With that experienced head, the matter must
Be tangled beyond hope, and deftly hid
That you cannot unravel and descry.

    One day ; another ; and another fled,
Yet came no Crito to Pygmalion,
Who, in the amber glow that warmed the
        fourth
At sunset mused,
             The poison bags were found
Harder to gather from the serpent fangs
Than Crito had believed. He hoped his friend
Would take no risk or insult in his zeal
To serve his well-beloved friend's only son !

So far had ambled on his thoughts when he
Beheld Lord Crito and Orsines both
Toward coming, Crito pale unwontedly.
  Taking the old man's hands, he asked

                                    How fares
My Lord, he lacks his wonted calm ?   And I,
Orsines, miss your customary cheer !

  Pygmalion, what I thought but clattering .
The wooden swords of youth in sportfulness,
I find no boy's play now ; but grip of steel
And deadly hate.   Murder is what they mean.

  Hate stealing on to murder : and for what ?

  That you shall hear ; and hearing have your
      mind
Expanded by the knowledge you shall learn.
  This youth of mine, whom now I find not quite
So innocent and simple as I thought,
Needed but feather touching to entice ·

His ugly secrets forth : for flippancy
And vanity combined to flatter him
He moved in matters of a high concern.

  It seems one Bacis with much care and pains
Made a design to show the Priests how he
Would run a frieze along their Temple walls:
And all declare Pygmalion's influence
Alone debarred the youth from just reward ;
Priests being favourable, Pygmalion not.
  They say that you keep haughtily aloof,
Mixing at no time in their games and feasts.
Likewise if one demand of you advice,
You give it plainly with no view to please ;
Unheeding that a statue-maker lives
As much by praise as food he takes in mouth.
In like wise this same Hebe you have made
Is some dark trick to serve the Mysteries.
And monstrous praises Priests and populace
Bestow on you belong of right to them.
Should this new art of stratagem succeed,

Inflaming people's taste with new disease,

Where can they find a market for their work ?

They are not rich enough they say, to dare

Murder young maidens and mix up their blood

With.clay, and thus to make their statues live !

Blood! Blood! they say must be atoned in blood;

The How, and When is silence ; we shall see !

When my glib youth had got thus far he

    stopped

Dead short and blushed.   I saw he went

    beyond

Intention ; from his loosened tongue had slipped

What he had fain concealed.   Then promptly I

Forbade all future intercourse between

Archaics and himself.   To make secure

I kept him to his chamber, guard at door :

Where he will stay till our needs call him forth.

None but a fool, or evil one will act

On news enormous without aid of sure

Supporting strength in proof.   I thought : then
    went
To seek this Bacis : found him squat amid
A gruff and grisly set in close discourse.
They ceased on seeing me, and with their eyes
Scowled their inquiries wherefore had I come ?
    As this was war I used my warlike arts ;
My youth, I told them wasted too much time,
And hoped they would not harbour him, as I
Had studies for my youth to learn that now
Were all or part neglected.   More of this
To same effect.   Then I began to note
The statues there on stands, and works on
    walls.
For all they cared my words might well have
    been
The outside wind that blew.   Lightly I passed
To this new Hebe of Pygmalion,
And lurid light so swiftly flew thro' all,
I almost heard the flashing of their eyes,
Showing how nearly lay the matter there.

It might be chance, but I young Bacis saw
· Fumble his sword-hilt lying close beside.
Then, no preliminaries, all at once
Began in rough loud tones to talk and shout
Of nothing but the weather, fish, and ships;
The costliness of wine with this last fail
Of grape.   I left them in a hot debate
If vintage or corn harvest made most gold.

Had Hades gaped and loosed her fiends, the
    cast
Were less destestable than this foul reek
Of midden heatedness and gutter slush !
    Lies are built up by liars pleasantly ;
They give their lies whatever form they please,
But ugly always.   On these shapes they stick
In flagrant spots a few bright specks of truth.
Forth wend the lies with maggot life endowed,
And multiply with such amazing speed,
Man's whole life from the cradle to the grave
Is plagued by wingèd ones, or lies that crawl.

And little as it takes to make a lie,
That lie may take a man's lifetime to kill.

   Of this same Bacis I will tell the tale.
Long since Orsines in athletic zest
Seeking young athlete of some small renown,
In quarters where our thieves and lowly dwell,
Saw sitting cross-legged by the gutter side
A sharp-eyed boy making men's heads in clay.
Orsines thought he had unearthed a gem
So rare it must be ground and fitly set
To edify mankind.   Orsines knew
My faith in baseborns weak ; but urged this
    gem
Was an exception, proved my rule was true,
For who before had known an ill-bred bird
Hawking at statues, that belong to Gods !
Fondly, reluctantly, I then agreed
To buoy his ardent whim, and sent the lad
Where best he might be taught the statue work.

   To those who know but little statue craft,
Who are, my Crito, nearly all we know,

His progress was a marvel.   He by work
Dexterously instinctive soon outran
By rapid ways the rest.   I tried to keep
Him in the ancient paths with no avail ;
As I foresaw he could no higher rise
Unless with broader base to build upon.
As chances came in many ways I gave
What   help   I   could   and   thought   he   lived
    content.

    When on Athena's Temple Priests proposed
To have some friezes carved, young Bacis sent
Designs of mortals going to sacrifice,
Which did not please them : but as Bacis said
The Lord Pygmalion would be gratified
Should they entrust him with their holy work
The High Priest thought best ask of me direct.

    I could in no way sanction such a feat
On any sacred fane.   It was grotesque,
Ridiculous.   Maidens with hanging jaws
Weak in the neck.   Men of thin breasts and
    arms,

But round the belly large ; short in the legs.

Throughout their lengths limbs almost of one
    size,

Ignobleness impressed on every part.

    For this must Bacis not the least be blamed.

He drew but what his eyes had mostly seen ;

Women so poor in blood their heads drop
    down ;

Showing the emptiest ignorance of life

In beings fit to share the sacrifice.

Men who lounge in the houses of their wares

All day, no exercises, do perforce

Grow unheroically stout.   And he

Having no inborn nobleness, or light

To compensate original defects,

And wanting also simple modesty

To feel and conquer birth deficiencies,

The end was such presentment as I say.

    To our chief potter I commended him

Who cheerfully gave work of comic heads

Fashioned to pots, and any odd device

His fancy might invent, which products would
Be taken in large numbers by the crowd ;
And thus appealing unto those he knew
Them he would gladden and enrich himself.
But guard the Gods I will from such as he.
I who would consecrate estate and life
To Gods could scarcely sacrifice the Gods
To profit Bacis.
                    Truly, Crito cried,
His tale is told.   All but Orsines know
A fish on land is but an awkward beast.
But fair to tell, when of these fishy freaks
Orsines heard, he vowed him every chance
To prove his fishy nature in the sea.

Yes, and had done so had you not forbade !

What mean these knaves that I mix in no
     games ?
I mix in every public game, and am
One of the Chiefs ; made one by better skill !

That I should mix in little games and feasts
Is the inanity of recklessness.
Those who have nothing have the fewest cares ;
But I have vineyards, corn countries, and
      woods ;
Store-houses, quays, an active fleet of ships ;
All which, tho' I have trusty heads, demand
Some thought of me, and that too, closely
      given.

Without your statues I should say you had
More than enough to keep the best at work.

Orsines, no : the more we have to do
Better we do it and more rapidly.
The mind beats into higher pace and flies
With less exertion winged at utmost speed.
    As to my giving plain advice when asked,
I never treat these knaves but as I wish
These knaves to treat me should I ask advice ;
And, save in fortune, which is luck of wheel,

Had shrunk from holding one of them as less
Than I myself am till I found them rogues.

   As to my praise, I utter all I can,
And cannot lie even to flatter knaves.
The dread their market may be spoiled by me
Is needless fear, the foolish are with them.

   Regarding this blood murder business, that
Might prove a sling in awkward slinger's fist.

   But loved Pygmalion make us promise you
Will not walk public ways without your sword.

   Promise I make, let that content you both.

BOOK XI.

PYGMALION walking toward the Council Hall
Where other two with him were pledged to
    choose
A plan for its embellishment, his gaze
Lay on the azure of a laughing sea,
A sapphire ending shade-divided street.
Till, hearing ring of coming chariot wheels
He turned and saw Crito with Graceless pass
At speed ; but not too fast for Crito's glance
Of greeting ; when, but not till then, he found
He had forgot his promise and his sword.

After debate had ripened into choice
The Judges three had left the Council Hall.
Pygmalion striding homeward met midway
Crito who walked alone.

Your just rebuke
Most surely earned have I ; but pray before
You hurl your bolt on my offending head
Hear how that head has failed of its intent.
    Zealously striving to obey commands,
My sword I shifted from its wonted place
To hang on nail I drove into the door
Leading from my workchamber ; so that I
On leaving must perceive it.   But to-day
The heat being great I set the door ajar,
So leaving saw it not.   Now I recall
A jingling made as I closed fast the door,
Which then seemed strange ; but being too
        much urged
To keep my hour for scrutiny, it passed
Outside remark.

Pardoned you must be now,
But sin no more.   In these deep shades let us
Clasp that fair creature Chance and taste her
        sweets.

She is too shy that pretty Wantonness ;
So hold her fast, embrace her while we can.

In abler hands I now will leave the sword
Until conviction forces grip of hilt.

Now we will argue out the murder plot.
Why do you think my senses are deceived ?

Nay, not deceived O Crito ; over-keen !

A common form to call his sight too keen
Who sees beyond the caller !   Then am I
A boy full-sail, no ballast in my hull,
No steersman at the helm ; I drive so fast
Perhaps on rocks and ruins ?

                              No, no ; not so.
But men may hate and do dire deadly ill,
And yet stop short of murder foul and red.

Tracing the spirit through its various shapes
In law and custom takes long time to learn.

Who learns will often see no difference
Between an act the law rewards with death
And one the law regards with stone blank eyes.
A lazy rascal, drunken and half starved
Scatters a rich man's brains and steals his purse:
There is no question what becomes of him.
A hard stern parent has a gentle child
Whom, from moroseness, or some cause obscure
He hates ; and with fixed purpose day by day,
By savage looks, harsh words, and heartless
    thwart
Crushes her soul thro' wretchedness to death.
What law or custom interferes with him ?
And yet a knife drawn thro' her tender throat
Were mercy's self compared with that long
    death
She died !

      Too true ! I had not thought of this,
Which now too clearly sets in unveiled glare
The Cretan's fate, bluff Gortys. Every work

Of his was wild with fire, almost beyond
What statues should admit ; but lacked the
    round
Soft sweetening of parts which captivates,
Thus lacked sweet-sucking people's sweet sup-
    port :
Seeing him surely sliding out of fame
The wolfish pack set on him ; headed him ;
And at the turns snapped their remorseless
    bits ;
Never removing bright determined eyes,
Or slacking pace till they had pulled him down.
   This demon hunt was not achieved with jaws
Blood red from snaps of flesh.

                  The hunt was made
By merry jokes ; light, but well-aimed pooh-
    poohs ;
Made while they drank their wine at rich men's
    boards,
When no one could suspect of spite or hate.
So happy were they ; in such playfulness !

See how they laugh ! Note what embittered
  things
They bandy round against their cheerful
  selves,
But bitter legless things that fall.   Unlike
Their pretty ridicules, which sharp-hooked, stick
And make the victim bleed.
                              Yes, Crito, now
I see the spirit may be one with his
Who slays with sling or sword, and citizen
Who sleekly marks one helpless to his death
By means concealed securely from the dull.
And what the dull ones fail to understand
Borders on folly in the wise to show.

This pack, Pygmalion, joining in one cry
Could not by howling hunt you out of life ;
From this you are as far removed as stars.
They cannot pinch your heart to starving death ;
They know not how to poison you ; therefore
Will use their only remedy at hand.

As loved Pygmalion now you see their souls
Can you doubt longer these men mean your
    death ?

  I do not doubt their meaning, but I doubt
Their power to execute. You scarcely think
They could make civil war to murder me ?

  I do not fear a war ; but much I fear
An ambush. This my care you should not go
Swordless about the ways. For well I know
A few of these same knaves were but a stroke
Of play for your unerring sword to give
Them lasting peace: unarmed, Pygmalion, think!

  I do not much affect the sword you know,
Compared with bow and spear; for one takes skill
Of poise in handling ; while the other flies
A venture with the wind. But with my sword
Crito, give me a high wall at my back
Six of these wretches would find overwork

To touch me ; and it would go hard indeed
Did I not thin the circle.   Warriors born
Fight with their feet as much as with their
    hands :
It is the thrust, and backward leap that tell ;
The certain eye that makes each stroke a
    death,
Or limb disabled ; and the cold clear brain
That odds can never fluster.

                   All most true,
And therefore wear your sword !

                  Pygmalion found
On reaching home the weight of Crito's threat
To leave the sword in abler hands than his.
For when Ianthe, waiting, saw him pass
Toward his work-chamber, straight she sought
    him there,
Her visage all aglow with eagerness,
A boon my Lord ; I crave a boon of thee !

Ianthe could not ask what was not mine
To give ; and therefore waiving question I
Grant your desire.   Yea, tho' it were to snare
A lion and bring netted to your feet.

Swear then by Aphrodite, and by Zeus,
You will not leave your home or work-chamber
Without a sword safe buckled by your side!

I see, his dread on you has Crito laid ;
Gladly I swear by Aphrodite, Zeus,
And every God that sways our mortal life ;
And if I durst would swear by Styx itself.
But O, my Treasure, had I sworn by you
The thread of Fate could not have bound me
        more.

The Maiden's soul now bright and   satis-
        fied,
She would have left him to his silent Gods
Had not his love delayed her.   In his arms

He took her wealth of loveliness, and kissed
Her answering lips.

                Too fair, too fair for man
To call his own of right Ianthe thou !
By what strange blessedness to me is given
A form that moves Olympian in its grace !

    A time will çome when wars will rage and
      clash
Harsh thunders thro' the land. At such a time,
Amid the crash my place will be to bind
The heat of battle into fire and burn
A ruthless entrance in the foeman's strength.
Should some malignant dart, or deathful blade
Check me in sudden night, you will recall
The best Pygmalion had to give was thine ;
The best Pygmalion ever knew, thy love.

    Since Aphrodite in Her graciousness
Had given Pygmalion his undreamed Delight,
And as an easy following consequence,
The power to make his statue live and gaze

Awestruck before the awful face of Zeus,
He had a lover's fondness for the walls
Of Her great Temple standing proud and clear,
A brightness in the day ; a gloom at night,
Save where the roof or column edges took
The sprinkling light of stars or of the moon.

    Most often would he when the palace slept,
Save for the guards who paced at intervals,
Go forth alone and wander in the shades
Or open spaces round the Temple, where
Foxes and wolves had watched and taken note.

    He fed delightful fancies as he moved ;
At every step some lovely memory
Justled the lovely one that came before ;
And each fresh comer made his heart more glad.

      He wondered what so long could cloud his
        sight
Against Ianthe's beauty, grace, and love ;
For love with both must long have been at point
Of bursting to the full and perfect flower.
Was it his struggling to achieve the life

And put a soul in statues made him blind;
As one in battle would not heed the gleam
Of sudden glory on a mountain side;
Would only feel the glitter in his sight,
Or see a vantage if it smote the foe's?

    How earnestly she came to crave her boon.
Her hands down-clasped their utmost length
    before :
The lift of her sweet face supplicating!
In those deep eyes the droop of tenderness!
Her radiance when the sacred oath was given!
    How prettily she buckled on my blade;
Passing her hand atwixt the belt and me
To find if drawn too tight!   Could I forget
An oath so asked, so gladly vowed? Not while
This head commands my motions: while this
    sword
Is mine to wear
            Ah ! Ha !
                He happily

Held scabbard in his hand, for on him rushed
From   out   the   darkness   three   with   naked
     swords.
   Pygmalion was a muser ; but the woods
No leopard held with senses more alert ;
No leopard's backward spring could be more
     quick
And sure than his when he beheld their blades
Lifted to strike.   Unsheathing at the pause,
An instant, and he forward leaped ; a swift
Dark gleam, a groan ; but ere the body fell
A clash, another gleam, and dismal shriek
Pierced ghastly thro' the silence of the night
And both slain fell together ; while the third,
Nerveless for terror at their hasty fate,
Turned round and fled.   Pygmalion feared the
     chase,
For stones unhewn and shaped lay cast about,
With planks and blocks the Temple workmen
     used
In mending some defects at base, and threw

His sword, which caught the flying wretch
  between
The calf and tendon of the heel slantwise,
Whereat he would have fallen, had he not
Driven on a spearhead which Orsines held
Advanced to stop his flight.

                      Crito had learned
Pygmalion's nightly rambles, and had told
Orsines, who in shadows watched unseen
Night after night no harm befel his friend,
And now, on hearing clash and shriek, rushed
  forth
His spear at point, which, entering Bacis just
Below the breast, ended his flight for life.

  When at Pygmalion's call torches were
  brought
By guards on watch, they showed the first who
  felt
The blade was the same athlete, now grown
  huge
And strong, Orsines sought in days agone :

The other was a swordsman of the best
In Cyprus, and among Archaics thought
Pre-eminent in statue-making craft :
And Bacis lay with both hands clutching hard
The fatal spear ; and on his features death
Had glazed the eyes and fixed a grin of pain.

When the dark story of those murderous three
Was noised abroad, Pygmalion shone like day.
The clouds dispersed ; the wild winds fell; his
    praise
Was trolled by every tongue. What could show
    more
Our age's madness than that men should rave
Against Pygmalion, just, and strong, and wise ?
All always knew some harm would come to those
Who dared assail his lofty name with spite.
How happy he could guard his life so well !
For had his priceless thread been cut what loss
To Cyprus : how the King had grieved ! And his
Poor Hebe statue, what must that have felt ?

Those silly nobles who had snapped the lies
That swarmed and buzzed around Pygmalion's
　　name,
Heard the crowd singing and sang with the
　　crowd
Their abject adulation.
　　　　　　　　　　Pottery men
Fashioned his likeness on their drinking-cups ;
And there were plots to have a statue made
To show how Cyprus could adore her great.
　　The minstrels unto gaping crowds forth
　　　poured
In floods Pygmalion's almighty deeds,
The doing which had taken ten long lives ;
Achilles not more brave, Alcides strong ;
And a moot question if Prometheus self,
Or even Hephaestus could have wrought a form
That breathed a sweeter life than Hebe's smile.
And some gave murky hints they were not
　　　sure
He could not roll the thunders an he pleased !

And thus from baseless calumny the herd
Of rich and poor, thoughtless as sheep that bleat,
Passed into senseless ecstasy of laud ;
As din of croaking frogs melodious,
Or deafening caws that rend the evening air.

BOOK XII.

THE prodigy, three murderous wretches slain
By two great Chiefs of war, was yet alive
In idle tongues, when drifting rumours shook
Both weaklings and strong men throughout the
    land.

    The rumours threatened Egypt would avenge
Her overthrow some twenty summers past ;
For the last Pharaoh in his death-hour claimed
This promise of his son, who sternly swore
By their remorseless Gods he soon should hear
From ghostly messengers in shadow world
That Cyprus was their own ; that the one son
Of him who led the war was led in chains
For mockery in old Egypt's capital,
    In smiles the aged Pharaoh closed his life,

Hearing the cries of future victories.
For when that broken enterprise returned
His thwarted rage had doomed to death the
     Chief
Who marched his armies to their fall, but was
Of all his Lords the one he favoured most,
Revenge thus sweetly soothed him as he died.

The ships were coming in from every sea;
Their hordes were arming fast; they would be
     thrown
Wave upon wave in hungry multitudes
Cyprus could raise no forces to resist.

Such were the rumours that appalled the
     land
With certain conflict and conjectures wild.
While freaked with terror labour ran astray.
The tiller ploughed his furrows all awry;
Wide of her bowl, the cow-girl milked the
     ground;

Swineherds drove swine to feed with pastured
    sheep,
And sheep were driven in the swineries.
The armourer burnt his metal gossiping,
And merchants could not make their balances.
The gilded idlers, erst of fluent prate
And buzzing nothings, nothing had to say.
While silent men now stormed in fiery speech
Threatening the throngs on crowded quays and
    ways
They would be slain, or slaves, unless they
    sprang
Straightway to savagery in slaughterous war,
Where each must feel an overmatch for three !

From merchants flying home in rapid ships,
Men of renown and weighty in the state,
The King and Rulers learned that Egypt
    swarmed
Alive with preparation, ships and men
Bound to make Cyprus vassal of her sway.

N

Time now was more than life.   To choose a
    Chief
In whom authority be absolute
To hold the force of Cyprus at his will,
In this they saw their first necessity.

The King and Rulers met in Council Hall,
And as the King said each Lord present knew
Wherefore they met, he asked them to propose
Without delay the Chiefs to be discussed.

Pygmalion !   Crito !   Our Orsines !   Loud
Were called from every side, and these alone.
    The King then asked,

                    Crito as first in age
And deep experience, will you be Chief,
Should your name bear the heaviest lot in votes ?

My knowledge and my sword are yours, O King,
And will be used in service.   Now, alas !
I own not that reserve of manhood's strength

Needed to hold our forces in control
During this imminent and dreadful stress,
And therefore for Pygmalion give my vote.
   The King next asked,

                    Orsines, should the weight
Of votes fall to your name, would you be Chief?

   O King, I must refuse, for well I know
Another better fitted to command.
Our island, after Crito, holds no head
So clear and wise ; no one whose skill so great
In war ; no arm so strong to execute
As our Pygmalion's.   Him I give my vote.

   Pygmalion, cried the King, as all the votes
Are yours you must accept the Chieftainship,
And during this dark crisis imminent,
Hold all our power in trust to meet the foe.

   As you, O King, and these your ruling Lords,
Lay on me this great charge I must obey.

With Crito and Orsines, rest content,
The swarms of Egypt will not range the Isle
After the fashion of a pleasure jaunt !
   No foe could come more welcome to these
      arms.
Beating these nation-gorgers off our shores
My Father met his fate.   By sacred Zeus,
I swear ; by all the Gods of highest heaven,
To claim full payment for the debt they owe.

   Uprose the King, supported on each side,
And passed out from the Council Hall.   With
      pain
The Rulers saw how lustreless his eyes ;
How wan his wrinkled visage : bowed and sunk
Those shoulders once so signed by kingliness
His subjects cast their bearing after his.

   Swiftly the tidings flew Pygmalion held
The forces of the island in command.
And all the nation as at rise of sun

Woke at a bound in buoyancy and joy.

The tiller now could plough his furrows straight,

But left the plough to flourish spear and shield.

The cow-girl now could fill the frothing bowl.

The shepherd and the swineherd left to boys

Due care of sheep and swine.   The armourer
    now

No metal spoiled, but wrought unceasingly

A merry tune that gladdened hearers' hearts.

The merchants, girding on their warlike swords,

Boasted their balances must bide their time.

And gilded idlers plunged in discipline,

While the roused silent cried exultingly,

Their dearest hopes were coming truths at last!

    From every part the Chieftains gathered men

Who crowding came, unasked, to take the toil

Assigned them in the now fast mustering hosts.

Nimbly from chariots strong lances flew,

And all day eager bowmen practised aim ;

The spearmen knelt in low straight even lines

In four or five ranks deep behind their shields,

Their points at moving threat, each beyond each;
Or at a word the whole as one would rise,
And bounding forward rush in mimic charge,
Then drawing backward sink again to rank.

Pygmalion knew the woodmen of the Isle,
Dexterous in use of axe ; a stubborn race,
Clad in hard leather fitting to their shapes,
And formed them one rough body who would
    dare
Make their attack uncovered by a shield.

He built tall towers of wood, huge wheels
    inside
Which twelve strong men could push and move
    at will ;
A platform roofed atop for chosen bows
Whose arrows carried fate.
                        The training ceased
Not even with the dusk at setting sun.
In the wild heat of infinite commands

Crito forgot his age : his eyes and voice
Were everywhere giving young leaders help
Of ancient wiles for safety and attack.
While everywhere Orsines checked the rash,
And stayed the eager by his steadiness.
No need for inspiration, all were fire.

Men watched from every height along the
    coast ;
Ships from all quarters hastened into port ;
Save flying vessels sent to catch the first
Glimpse of the foe and bring the tidings home.

Awhile the fleets of Egypt had been bound
In idleness by winds, and adverse storms,
One hard on other's heels ; such, old men
    said,
Had not been known on Egypt's seas before.
And every hour was Cyprus' gain. At length
A ship that had outsped the rest was seen
Nearing the shore and signal made the Foe.

Straightway Pygmalion summoned every
    Chief
Who could be spared from guarded points,
    and care
Of raw and youthful ranks, to make them know
His battle-plan.
                    He meant the foe to land ;
Slingers and archers from safe vantage spots
To greet the landing with unceasing showers
Of stone and steel : but when the landing swelled
To vasty numbers backward must they fall
On the main battle by the ways they knew.

    He meant the battle to be shaped like that
Which his lost Father fought. He meant them
    not
Move one pace from their stations till he cried
The general onset, when his whole wedge would
Steadily open to a level line
Resistless driving Egypt in the sea.

    He meant the chariots not to charge in force
During the onslaughts of the foe ; but hang

And hover in two bodies near the horns
To stop the hordes from taking them in rear :
Should any chance surprise make this a dread
The axemen in reserve must fill the gap.

Having made clear his plans to every Chief,
Pygmalion then dismissed them to their posts,
Save Crito and Orsines who remained.

He who has fought in many battlefields
Knows during heat and press of action will
Arise such dangers unexpectedly
As must tax all the wisest head can know
To give them counter-check : therefore do I
Leave nothing at a hazard I can guard.
And you my two best friends have each to share
A deed I dare not trust to other hands.

Orsines you will have your ships in port
Ready as hounds are when unleashed to slip
And charge their vessels from the seaward side
With shafts, and fire, and drive them on the
      shore

When on this mound between the beach and
    town
You see my signal smoke and fire arise.
    As the destruction of these enemies
In any satisfying way depends
On this great signal telling time exact
To him who holds the fleet, I must the task
Intrust to you, O Crito : you alone.
Six runners will I send you following ;
But when the second reaches, fire.   The rest
Are but to make security more sure.
    Glaringly manifest the flaming pile
Then, with all spears and chariots you com-
    mand
Attack on right of me, for I shall then
Be pressing on with my whole force in line.

    Proudly at eventide the Pharaoh's fleet,
Innumerable, and unmolested, lay
Threatening in dreadful beauty off the shore.
A flood of glory from the stormy west

Poured over dancing waves and splashed the
    ships
With antic gold ; and drove dark purple shades
Far on the waters to the deepening East.

  All night on every point along the shore
Burned signal watchfires ; watchers each in turn
Taking his rest.   Fresh must be every man
To-morrow's dawn, for every man awakes
The fate of Cyprus holding in his hands.

  When last from darkness feeble pallors broke
Pygmalion peering thro' the glimmering saw
Movement among the ships, and straight gave
    word
To rouse the host.   Fiercely then squealed the
    pipes,
And hoarsely brayed the sea-shell trumpeters :
The army like a monster myriad-voiced
Sprang into instant life, the tramp of men,
The shouting leaders, metal clang of arms.

His host of axes, chariots, spears, and bows,
Pygmalion formed between the city walls
And sea, far lying, on wide stretch of ground,
The forward spur of some great inland range,
And, like his battle lines, wedge shaped ; down-
    sloped
On every side but that towards the town.

He placed a stout-built, bow-armed, wooden
    tower
At either horn of his great battle wedge ;
Three near the point to bear the heaviest brunt ;
Five on his Eastern side, at intervals,
Two on the West ; being steeper there, the
    chance
Of onslaught less.

                    Well posted, Crito held
His mound.   The pile of pine-boughs resinous,
Damp heaps of leaves on oil-soaked flax : and
    men
With torches ready to obey the word,
Were guarded by his chariots and spears.

Grim in reserve before the city gates

The axemen resting on their glittering blades.

On each flank trembling in a splendour-blaze

The brazen chariots mocked the risen day ;

Their neighing horses pawed, and strained the reins

Impatient to be thundering thro' the land.

Orsines with Pygmalion traced the lines,

Trimming the men and cheering, till afar

They saw the arrow-showers by the shore

Glisten like webs in dewy mornings bright,

And hitherward the archers falling back

Before their ever-thickening enemy ;

When crying

        Ships ! Orsines to your ships.

Charge from the open, drive their fleet ashore !

Pygmalion left him.

        Plunged the tide of war :

The flying bows now slipped within the lines,

Driven by the raging swarm, whose points so fast

Began to sprinkle helm and shield, he brought

His bowmen into rank behind the spears,
Bidding them answer rapidily and sure.

Like ramping waves upon a bar of rock
The hot Egyptians dashed upon the wedge,
And like the ramping waves fell broken back.
But when successive onslaughts baffled, beat
Their ardour to a pause, shouted the Chief,

Three spear-lines charge, and back again to rank!

Forth rushed the triple line with levelled points
And smote the battle such a shock their scream
Of horror tore the thunderous air.   When back
Again at threat.
                    Now bows, Pygmalion said,
Play me a merry tune !
                              The volleys whizzed,
Whistling the airs of death.

                              Is that the air
You play me ?   Half the shafts fly overhead ;

The rest strike nowhere! Rabbits; Geese, I
   say.

Aim you between the navel and the breast.

Nay, not so keen. If no bare places show

To let your arrows in, then wait and watch

The chance. Aim at the face no farther off

Than ten fair strides; then, between mouth and
   brow.

   Well shot, my men. Now you are lions : yea,

And leopards beautiful.

                Tower there! Behold

That tall-capped chieftain ; he fights much too
   well ;

Down with him. Ha! He staggers ; throws
   out spear

At nothing ; falls!

           They crowd, and boldly press

Our eastern horn ; signal the chariots!

But stay ; so thick they fall around the tower

We may not need them. Chariots I want fresh

Ere long to join the chase.

Strange ; no charge I see
Against our lines, what means it, can you tell ?
Pygmalion of a bold young leader asked.
  The bold young leader thought the foe had
    fed
On Cyprian darts, and Cyprian spears enough,
And would be glad to end the feast and go.

  Then must we stuff them if they will not eat !
I see it now ; my towers have deftly done
Their work too well for Pharaoh's host, and
    slain
Most of their leaders ; for I gave the word,
Unless hard driven, as that Eastern tower,
Those bowmen were to slaughter none but
    chiefs ;
This makes their hesitation ; easy now
And golden-paved our way to victory.
  Send my six runners off to Crito now !
Command the axes to come slowly down
With every flanking chariot east and west.

I see a black storm rising from the south
Will wash our dusty visages and make
A puddled fighting ground.   My work begins !

Fiercely   the   storms   had   Crito's   mound
    assail'd,
And he had burned to bind his force and charge
Headlong and crush the fiery foe with spears :
Mindful of fire and pile, he dared no more
Than beat off each assault.   O Pygmalion,
He sighed, how coldly clear that planning brain !
Who with a head less calm and reverent
To warlike strict obedience than mine
Could have forborne the temptings of this day ?
    Gazing he saw Pygmalion's western wing
Straightening towards the mound ; and while
    he gazed
A runner coming crying, Crito, Fire !
Another close at heels, whom, ere he made
The mound, an arrow struck and felled : one
    more,

O

Nigh stumbling over him, ran in and cried
Fire, my Lord Crito, fire the pile !   At once
All torches kissed, and with their flaming tongues
Licked at the feast of oil and resinous gums.
Great grew the flames and roaring caught the
    leaves
That sent a thick gray smoke high in the air.
  Then Crito shouted

                  Chariots to right,
Flank the Egyptians, drive them eastward back.
Spears form in triple line ; press on to join
Pygmalion's wing that fast is drawing nigh.

  Pygmalion's   Mother   on   the   gate-tower
    watched
Remembering.   At the King's wish she came
With Eos and Ianthe : sad herself
She strove to cheer him on this fateful day.

  All day the fight had seemed some monstrous
    thing

Hugging the earth and shuddering thro' its
    length.
And all day long they heard a sound as of
Far waters rushing over broken stones.

   The south grows black, tell me Ianthe what
Your younger sight can see ;
                        Bade the old King.

   Upon the mound a giant signal fire
Throwing a world of smoke. And chariots
    thronged
Driving at speed toward the western shore.
Now outward move the two great battle-lines.
And widely stretch across the plain and join
A line of spears that touches on the mound.
Now moves the whole line straight from west
    to east,
As I have seen an eagle spread his wings
Poising for prey. The chariots of both flanks
Are moving separate ways. The axes too

Are striding forward ; on their shoulders shine
The dreadful blades.

I see our ships far out
Now turning round towards the Pharaoh's fleet.

Orsines !   Eager Eos cried, how dares
He with that scanty sail of ships attack
A fleet so vast, enormous, as the foes' ?

Hard is it child to say, the King replied,
What that may be Orsines does not dare,
If bid by me, or by Pygmalion charged !

Be calm, the Matron said, for rest assured
Pygmalion had not sent his friend beloved
On service of more risk than man could take.
Behold !   Behold !   By the high Powers of
        Heaven
The Pharaoh's fleet is fired !   Again behold !
Our chariots thunder to the charge ; they catch
Them either wing.

Their fleet smoke clouds themselves.
But look, the axes are at work ; they rise,
And fall, and gleam like beat of seabirds' wings,
Incessant : every stroke must be a back
Hewn through, or head and helmet crushed. I
       scarce
Can see them now for smoke and flames beyond.
Escape for Egypt none. Slaves will be had
For asking, as they cannot kill the whole,
Their arms will ache too much.

                    Behold, then cried
Ianthe ; list that dreadful thunder roll !
Fighters and foes must both be overwhelmed ; ,
Stroke upon stroke the lightning lashes them !
The hungry tempest gapes to swallow all !

Look, Eos shrieked, our fleet is out at sea
And strives against the wind ; Orsines must
Be drowned. Thus to fight against Boreas,
And Zeus, and great Poseidon on the waves !

Eos my tender dove, thy birdlike head
Lay on this heart of mine ; and I will stroke
It into quietude, the old King said ;
Orsines could not play a wiser game
Than throw himself upon the open sea.
Their fleet on fire ; wind setting towards the
        shore,
Theirs he well knows a dangerous neighbourhood.
Rarely are Zeus, Poseidon, Boreas
Incensed against the brave.   If he can make
The harbour
            Ha ! what ails you man ? speak out !
Your face looks flying from an enemy,
So staringly your eyes start in advance !

The Chief, O King, a message from the Chief.

Send up the message !
                    And the message came,
And kneeling down before him, said, Dread
        King,

Pygmalion's reverent love, he bids me say
The enemy is beaten ; all his ships
Are burnt or driven ashore. The slaughter great,
And had been greater but their Chief was slain ;
When, losing heart, the rest laid down their arms.

Good, said the King, but why not captive
          make
Of that Egyptian Chieftain, was it chance ?

Pygmalion would have saved the Chief, but
          one,
A spearman, whose son wounded fell, and who
Was after coldly mangled, rushed and clove
The Chieftain's neck in twain ; he could not
          live,
He said, without this offering to Fate.
Pygmalion bade me add, himself, O King,
Anon would follow my report.

                              And while
He spoke the warm air trembled to the sound

Of chariots thundering up at topmost speed,
Leaving a storm of coiling dust behind ;
For unfulfilled, the threatened drench had passed
And left the evening bright.

                  Pygmalion, Lo !
He comes outstripping guards ! Ianthe cried,
His helm, sun-smitten, crowns him with a star !

   And while she spoke the thunder suddenly
Stopped at the gates below, changing to din
Of jingling arms ; the snort, pawing of dust,
And shaking of the chariot horses ; when,
Ere they could wonder, filling all regard,
Pygmalion entering fell before the King,
And took his long white withered hands to kiss,
And in the King's lap sank his stately head.

  My Son ! my Son ! How ? How ?
                Then checked, and bent
His aged face, and clasped him lovingly,
And muttered,

More than son.   Yea more ! yea more !
And lay so long in silence that at length
The Matron gently lifting up his face
Saw he had fainted.

                Soon by chafe and art
He was brought back to life ; Pygmalion then,
As if the King had been a suckling babe,
Carried him tenderly adown the steps
And placed him on his waiting litter, when
They bore him to his palace where he slept.

  Covered you are from head to foot in blood
Pygmalion ; are you hurt ? the Matron asked.
  Mostly Egyptian blood you see, my own
Dear mother.   I had not a scratch until
The general onslaught, when I sometimes felt
As I have often when in boyhood I
Among the brambles scrambled for their fruit,
Orsines holding cap for me to fill.

  Now will I to my bath and make me fit
To stand before your presence.

                              Eos asked,
Is a great victory a glorious thing?

   O Eos nay!   It is more horrible
Than anything beside except defeat!

   Ianthe then,

                    Think O my dear One, think
Of those brave youths whose hands Pygmalion's
        clasped;
Whose lips have smiled upon him, cold in death.
Their mother's hopes all withered at the root!
The women who have lost their strong supports:
The children's wail for what will never come.
Such are the flowers that bloom where victory
Has soaked the earth in blood.   But were that
        blood
The well-shed blood alone of enemies
Then victory were in truth a glorious thing.

   The overwhelming blow his arms had struck

Egyptian arrogance had overthrown
The remnant of the old King's strength in joy.
His forces would not rally ; for, said he,
The dry shrewd son of Esculapius,
There are none left to call ; they gave his age
Their long farewells and left fareills instead.
In Council Hall guiding his ruling Lords
He never will sit more.

     ' The only cheer
Could soothe him was to have Pygmalion by :
For as he lay and clasped those mighty hands
Within his trembling own, he felt a hold
On life.

    I should not dread my fate, he moaned,
So much I long for rest : could I but know
The crown of Cyprus safe upon your head !

  And when the aged King's last hour had
   come, ·
Reverent and sad, around the chamber walls,
And silent sat the rulers, lacking hope.

His head lay resting on Pygmalion's breast;
Hands holding hand he sighed his latest breath,

Kingly art thou. O take my crown; my
    crown.

Before the King's sepulchral rites began
The Council, Crito told Pygmalion, would
Elect him King.   But, as they something knew
Of moodiness in him, and strange disdain
Of what the most held dear, right was it
    judged
To test beforehand would he take the crown
If his election stood by force of votes?

O tempter Crito!   What a net is this
You wind about me!   How can I resist?
Should I refuse and things go wrong henceforth,
On my unhappy head will lie the curse!
If I accept, ah then a long farewell
To what in me is dearer far than life

Without it ; making the similitudes
Of the great Gods I fear, love, and adore.

   We are but parts of what we dwell amidst ;
And if the press diverts us from our course
Helpless are we, and must submit, tho' sad,
And we look longing backwards evermore,
But I will ask Ianthe ; what she says,
So balanced am I, what she says I do.

   Then Crito went his way, mournful at heart
For loss of his loved King ; but pleased to
      know
Ianthe had the choice, as her great soul
Would choose the rugged path for him she
      loved.

   Crito was sent in all due form of state
Demanding, should the votes declare me King,
Would I accept their burden of the crown ?
I would give neither nay, nor yea, till you
Ianthe had avowed your will to me.

Trouble and sorrow greet me every turn :
No words can tell how my bewildered mind
Ran darkling while I strove to put the soul
In Hebe's statue.   Being done, arose
A swarm of loathly scandals till I slew
Their origin ; when burst and raged a din
Of nauseous flattery from the very knaves
Who used their skill to foul my name before.

My hard fate next forced these reluctant hands
To work this dreadful carnage, and behold
My friends in numbers dead as the cold earth
On which their bodies lay.   Then my blessed
     King,
Whom my soul loved as he had been a God,
Passed from me in these arms.   And now the
     Lords
Of Cyprus will to weight me with their crown,
And ruthlessly to rob me of my peace ;
My work in which my spirit knows delight.
That I may never feel again the bliss
Of silence and of solitary hours.

O my Pygmalion, well you know that I

Feel with your joys, and grieve with your
regrets.

Bitter the pain to wrench yourself from what

Your soul has cleaved to since the golden
days ;

The blossoming energy of youthful prime !

But they, meseems, whom most the great Gods
love

Are taken early from this battle-world,

Or have the heaviest burdens on them laid ;

Sometimes beyond their strength.   This is their
way

Of love ; not man's ; but we to them must bow.

If all the Rulers, all the best we know,

Demand the sacrifice, it is the Gods

Who speak by them.   We dare not disobey.

The greater loss, and greater pain, more
sure

The proof of its necessity.   The Gods

Are hard, relentless ; may not be denied.

A rugged path Pygmalion has to tread ;
But in his home there will be peace and calm.
He knows the Gods are just.   Let that suffice.

' At Crito's call the Lords of Council met
In solemn state and chose Pygmalion King.

'THE END.

Printed by R. & R. CLARK, *Edinburgh.*